I0606496

WOMEN OF THE LIVING DEAD

NOW AVAILABLE AND COMING SOON FROM OPEN CASKET PRESS

RATS
ASHES IN HER EYES
HEADSHOTS ONLY
ATOMIC ZOMBIES
ZOMBIE BUFFET
BIGFOOT TALES
HORROR CARNIVAL
CREATURE FEATURE
DEAD CHRISTMAS
DECAY: A ZOMBIE STORY
ZOMBIE BED & BREAKFAST (ZEE BEE & BEE)
HORROR TALES AND TERRIFYING STORIES
2012 ZOMBIE WALL CALENDAR
HOLLOW POINT: A ZOMBIE NOVEL
WARRIORS OF THE APOCALYPSE: BOOK 1
MUTANT APOCALYPSE
EARTH'S END

WOMEN OF THE LIVING DEAD

EDITED BY
JODY ANN GIANGREGORIO

Women of the Living Dead

Copyright © 2012 Open Casket Press

ISBN Softcover ISBN 13: 978-1-61199-045-4
ISBN 10: 1-611990-45-9

All rights reserved.

Open Casket Press is an imprint of Living Dead Press.
ww.livingdeadpress.com

All stories contained within this book have been published with permission from the authors.

No part of this book may be reproduced or transmitted in any form or by any means, electronic or mechanical, including photocopying, recording, or by any information storage and retrieval system, without permission in writing from the copyright owner.

This is a work of fiction. Names, characters, places and incidents either are the product of the author's imagination or are used fictitiously, and any resemblance to any actual persons, living or dead, events, or locales is entirely coincidental. This book was printed in the United States of America.

For more info on obtaining additional copies of this book, contact:
www.opencasketpress.com

Table of Contents

THE LIVING DEAD AT PENDERGHAST MANOR

JULIANNE SNOW

Chester Penderghast was about as normal as the family business was ever going to allow him to be. At just over five and a half feet tall, already balding and displaying an expanding paunch due in part from his constant enjoyment of all things sweet, there was not much going on in his relatively young life. He had a decent job—not one that he particularly wanted—but the pay was good and there was no way he could ever get fired. Besides, it really was one of the only jobs available where he lived.

Chester worked for his father as a junior mortician at Penderghast Manor in a small town tucked neatly into the Canadian countryside. Penderghast Manor was the only business offering funerary services for all of the small towns and villages within the vicinity of it. The manor had been in the Penderghast family for the last five generations and Chester's father was hoping he could one day turn it over to him. Business was fairly steady, and being the only funeral home in the area definitely helped. Death had a way of sneaking up on the living. It was the only inevitable life event that one could expect—other than taxes.

The manor itself was a large, sturdy house in the middle of town. Its facade was a commandingly calm gray brick with a black roof. With the white wraparound porch, the house itself looked inviting. The only aspect of the property that informed what went on inside was the demure sign on the front lawn announcing its function: *Penderghast Manor — When The Time Comes, Let Our Family Take Care Of Yours.*

It was Chester's sole job to prepare the bodies of the locals for viewing, and ultimately burial. It was his father's idea; Chester needed to perfect the craft and the only way to do that was to practice. Business was fairly steady, so he was confined to the cool, mint-green tiled room containing three white porcelain tables tucked into the basement of the house.

Working on his own gave Chester plenty of time with his thoughts. Thoughts that ranged from what God really looked like to what made up the flavor profile of Dr. Pepper. Those random but utterly consuming thoughts were what helped to distract him from the bodies he worked on every day.

He found that ignoring them was easier than dealing with them for the most part. In his teens, he had once asked his father how he dealt with the dead: the voices, the incessant questions or requests that resulted and the struggle to get them to lie still on the cold porcelain as he worked on them. After that admission, Chester was required to see a psychologist.

Dr. Hampton didn't take him seriously either, and as a result, Chester was diagnosed with some attachment related mental disorder that, to this day, he couldn't even pronounce. The psychologist told his parents that growing up around the dead had likely caused Chester to view them as a sort of imaginary friend. His parents were assured that he would grow out of it eventually and should continue to ignore the problem as best they could.

The prescribed medications didn't help Chester's problem and he soon learned to stop sharing his encounters with Dr. Hampton; there was no way the psychologist was ever going to believe what Chester told him. It was a little scary for Chester, knowing that he had to face them alone. The only saving grace was that none of the dead had yet tried do him any physical harm. Mostly they just tried to get used to the feel of death and that they would soon be confined to a coffin six feet below ground where they would have to live out the rest of their days in solitary confinement.

But what actually occurs after death? Death is not completely final. There is something that remains once one's pulse stops; a consciousness, best described as an afterlife, continues.

There are a few that escape the eternal box. They are the faceless, nameless people that you sometimes pass on the streets. The ones that you ignore, or rather, forget to notice. Unlike the Hollywood version of the zombie mythos, they are unconcerned with consuming living flesh. Their main goal is to find a quiet place to exist until the moment their bodies completely give out on them. In some rare cases, they seek out living companionship and to an extent, respect.

The best known example is Joan Rivers; it's obvious to anyone that looks at her that she has had a lot of work done. Her intention was to give off the appearance that she's still alive, but nothing could be farther from the truth. The story that passes for accepted fact among those in the know is this: Joan passed away naturally in her home and upon reawakening decided to carry on as if nothing had happened. She had the money to pay for silence and preservation services.

There is a relatively larger number of the dead among the living and there are reasons they remain — somewhat — anonymous. Chances are you can already figure out just who they might be.

One of the great advantages to being dead is that you get to decide who you want to communicate with. It's like a switch of sorts. One minute you are just a regular corpse, but with a pulse of dead 'energy,' you become apparently — and in some cases terrifyingly — sentient. It is part of the reason that most people are utterly unaware of the existence of the dead. They just have no desire to share their existential challenges with the world at large.

The only time they come out of hiding is on Halloween or for annual Zombie Walks. Nothing beats being able to be yourself and congregate with other dead in the community. Besides, one of them inevitably wins 'Best Dressed' each and every time. It's just one of the perks of being dead. The gore factor is readily apparent from the natural decomposition process and if you can't use it for recognition at some point, what fun is it really?

The only thing that really sucks about being dead is the fact that when you were alive, you were unaware of what occurred after death. The Funerary Services sector is booming, and burial and cremation are the accepted methods for the disposal of your deceased loved ones. For most, the only time they really had left before burial was at the funeral home.

For some reason, Chester got the ultimate nod of acceptance from the dead. It was almost an instinctual thing with them. In Chester's presence, they acted as if nothing was amiss. As far as any of them were concerned, they still had a lot of time left on their clocks and it didn't seem to matter that most of it was going to be spent underground.

Naturally, some begged and pleaded with Chester to let them leave. Of course, there was no way he could ever have done such a thing. The families of the deceased were counting on the Penderghast family to prepare their dearly departed for everlasting burial. That didn't stop the recently deceased from trying, though. And try they did…

It was a dark Friday night when William McShane was delivered to Penderghast Manor. At seventy-six, he was the oldest playboy for many miles. He still had all of his own hair, despite the fact that it was now snowy white, and it was rumored by a number of the local ladies that his physique was something to behold. Even at his advanced age, McShane's body was strong and his skin taut, stretched over those lean muscles. It seemed out of character for someone of William McShane's age to look and act so young, but it was something that he had gladly paid for. Nothing was too expensive in his endeavor to remain young, vibrant and popular with the ladies.

Once Chester was alone with McShane's body—still ensconced in the black body bag—he started to struggle, a muffled voice demanding that he be released immediately. Knowing he would have to get on with his work at some point, Chester obliged, sliding the large zipper down the length of the thick, reinforced plastic. As soon as Mister McShane could extricate his hands, he pushed them out and sat up on the table.

"Do you have a cigarette, boy?" uttered the deep and smooth voice of William McShane. It was just one of his many admirable attributes.

"Mr. McShane, you really shouldn't be smoking, it's not good for your health," Chester said before he thought better of it. His announcement got a heady laugh from the talking corpse in front of him. That and an annoyed look.

"C'mon, my good boy! Why don't you go and make yourself useful? I rarely smoke these days but I figure what's stopping me now?" At that point, McShane was trying his best to get both of his legs out of the body bag, probably intending to get up and find a cigarette himself, as Chester appeared to have no intention of satisfying his request.

As the body bag crumpled to the floor, Chester got his first good look at William McShane. He stood next to the white porcelain mortician's table, stark naked, and it was very evident how the playboy had spent the last moments of his libertine life. The reports of the man's prowess had to be true. Even at seventy-six, it was evident he was able to function with or without the help of the little blue pill.

Chester blushed at the shamelessness of the man and rushed over with a white sheet to cover his engorged penis. While used to seeing the genitalia of the bodies that passed through Penderghast Manor, there was still something unsettling about one of the dead lacking even a modicum of modesty.

"Seriously, young man? I'm dead, for Christ's sake. I didn't care about my modesty in life, so why the hell would I care now?" McShane laughed as he let the white sheet fall to the floor. "Besides, it's not like you've never seen one before. So grow a set, kid, and get me that fuckin' cigarette!" His request was made in an angry tone of voice and Chester had no idea what to do. There was absolutely no way he would be able to explain cigarette smoke in the workroom should his father happen to come downstairs. McShane was going to have to do without, but there was no reason that he had to know just yet.

"Sir, if you could please just lie back down on the table, I'll get you a cigarette once we're done with what we have to do," Chester lied with the hint of a plea edging into his voice. He had no intention of satisfying the man's demand for a cigarette, but he had a lot of work to get through and he'd learned it was easier to work on a compliant corpse.

McShane regarded him from where he now stood, next to the bank of square doors on the far wall. Opening one, he pulled out the tray. On it laid a forty-something woman named Shelia Mott who was silently coming to terms with her new position in the world.

"Well, hello there!" McShane crooned, making it obvious that even in death, he was hell-bent on playing the role of the playboy he'd crafted and honed in life. "What's brought you here?"

"Car accident," she said matter-of-factly, not even opening her milky eyes to look at McShane. "If you could leave me…"

"Hey, babe, a car accident is rough," McShane interjected. "I've got something stiff that might make you feel better…" As his voice trailed off, he started to gyrate his hips in what Chester could only assume was meant to be a sexy dance of invitation. Mrs. Mott was not even interested enough at the offer to open her eyes. Seeing that McShane wasn't going to score with this one, he uttered a single derogatory word as he rolled her tray back into place and slammed her cooler door closed in frustration.

"Mr. McShane, that was highly unnecessary! I've found that most of the dead prefer to be alone with their thoughts at this stage. It's a lot to take in, especially knowing that you're going to be buried until you completely decompose," Chester admonished, revealing more at this point than he probably should have. He looked down as he felt McShane's eyes bore into him.

"Pardon? I don't think I heard that last bit correctly," McShane said, his tone relaying his annoyance and a small amount of fear.

"It's not important at this point, Mr. McShane. However, what's important is that I need to get you ready for your family and friends. You don't want them to see you like this, do you?" Chester's question seemed to stop the playboy for a moment, then he realized that there were five other silver doors that he had yet to open.

"Ecnie, meenie, minee, moe…" McShane rambled off, pointing at random doors before settling on one of them. As he opened it, to reveal another woman, he instantly crooned, "Hey, baby, how's death treating you?"

A shrill scream was his only answer. Georgia Tedesto had started to turn her head in the direction of the voice, only to find herself face-to-face with the aroused crotch of William McShane.

"That's not the answer I was hoping for but if I'm being honest, that's the reaction I get from a lot of women when they catch their first glimpse," he slyly chuckled, pushing his arousal closer to Mrs. Tedesto's face.

"Mr. McShane, stop that! It's inappropriate and crude." Chester was unsure of how else to stop him, but instinctively he knew that shame was as unlikely to work. He walked over to the bank of refrigerators built into the far wall and soothingly addressed Mrs. Tedesto, as he rolled her tray back inside. "I'm terribly sorry, ma'am, and I apologize for his crude behavior. Please forgive him; he's only just getting used to being dead." It was meant more as an apology than an explanation but it served both purposes quite nicely.

With Mrs. Tedesto safely stashed back into the wall, Chester turned his attention to William McShane as anger overtook his normally calm visage. "That was extremely uncalled for Mr. McShane, you really should be ashamed of yourself." While looking the playboy in the eyes, he knew the exact moment that the third stair from the bottom creaked under his father's weight. As McShane went limp, falling to the floor, Chester's father, the imposing James Penderghast, entered the room.

"I don't know how many times I've told you to stop talking to the guests." His sharp eyes took in the corpse on the floor by the mortuary coolers and Chester's hand still resting on a chrome handle. "What are you doing? Why is Mr. McShane on the floor? Jesus, Chester, I thought you had more respect for the dead than this…" His voice trailed off as he spied the full state of the body. Coming further into the room, he stated quite matter-of-factly, "You're going to have to tie that thing down. The family wants an open casket."

He placed his hands underneath McShane's arms and looked up at Chester. "Well, we haven't got all night. Are you going to help me or not?"

Sensing his father's exasperation and anger, he took hold of McShane's ankles and hefted the corpse onto one of the table with his father's help. His father went to the cabinet and withdrew his tools, returning to stand next to the body of the notorious playboy. He laid his tools out carefully on a smaller table equipped with wheels, making sure they were all accounted for. As he settled himself adjacent to the right shoulder of the prone corpse, he made the first incision to expose the common carotid artery and jugular vein, stretching them both gently out through the mouth of the incision. With the task completed, he began to prepare the proprietary embalming fluid they used for injection into the carotid while Chester worked the limbs and muscles of the corpse, relieving any latent rigor mortis still remaining. Before placing the modesty cloth over the exposed genitalia, Chester forced the playboy's erection downward and used a length of cotton string to tie it off to the left leg.

Chester and his father worked in silence, the soft rhythmic sound of the centrifugal pump the only noise in the room. He appreciated it when his father came to help him as it meant that the dead played dead for the duration of their tasks. Once the body had been properly embalmed, Chester transferred it onto the tray of one of the fridge compartments as his father prepared to leave.

As James Penderghast reached the door, he turned back to Chester and said, "Son, I know you don't like this job very much but playing games with the corpses is just creepy." With those final parting words, he climbed the stairs into the warmth of the kitchen.

Hanging his head in dismay, Chester started to push the metallic tray containing William McShane into the refrigerator, but before he could move the tray more than a few inches, a hand reached out to his right forearm and elicited a started gasp from Chester.

"I'm sorry, young man. I didn't mean to *grass you up* with your father. Now that I'm dead, I wish I'd treated my sons a little better." The cool hand squeezed Chester's arm in something akin to comfort, then dropped back to its previous position.

"Good night, Mr. McShane," Chester said, confused by the understanding shown to him by a man in McShane's position. At some point, his father would understand, Chester was sure of it. Eventually, he would see the error of his ways, only then it would be too late for him to change anything.

Closing the door to the long, horizontal fridge, Chester was glad his night would soon be over. Not that he had anything planned. The ladies tended to steer clear of him due to his profession. The general consensus in town was that Chester Penderghast was creepy.

He cleaned up the embalming room, making sure that all of the tools and surfaces were clean, then turned off the light. As he ascended the stairs into the kitchen, he could hear the muffled conversations occurring amongst the dead. It spoke to the fact that community was still important to them and it made Chester wonder if they could talk to each other while buried underground. Was it possible to carry on a conversation with your neighbor with a few feet of dirt separating you?

Later, after eating and showering and dressing for bed, this last thought rolled around his head as he fell asleep.

A sharp knock awoke Chester long before his alarm was set to go off. It was a knock that he was used to, always followed by his father entering the room. It was the same room that he'd grown up in, containing the same twin-sized wooden bed and Star Wars sheets.

"We have a new delivery in the basement that needs to be completed quickly, son," his father said. "The family wants the body ready for burial within the next twenty-four hours at the latest. And they're willing to pay for a rush job." These were the kinds of clients his father thrived on. They were willing to pay anything, especially if it meant they could get what they asked for, and in the time frame they demanded it in.

Putting on his work clothes, Chester made his way to the basement workroom, stopping in the kitchen only long enough to quickly swallow a cup of his mother's strong coffee. She smiled at him from the sink, where she was washing the dishes. He entered the workroom, surprised by the sight before him. On the largest of the three embalming tables lay two women. Only it wasn't two women. As Chester got closer, he could see that while they might be two women, they shared one body.

Well, almost one body.

From the waist up, everything was anatomically correct, but below the belt was where things got interesting. The women were joined together starting at the hip and shared one fused leg between them.

"I wonder how often they won the three-legged race at the fair?" his father quipped insensitively. Normally, the ideal of propriety and respect, the comment was completely out of character, throwing Chester off-guard for a moment.

As Chester stared at the bodies, he wondered how difficult it must have been to live like that. As a clumsy child with only two legs and one body to deal with, he couldn't fathom the obstacles they must have fought to overcome. Lost in his thoughts for a moment, his mind soon turned to the possible obstacles he might encounter while embalming the pair. Trying to work out his plan of attack in his head, he didn't hear his father addressing him.

"Chester! Hello?" his father shouted beside him to gain his attention. Once Chester turned his head in his father's direction, James continued "This is going to be a difficult case, no doubt about it. But we need to get it done quickly. I've got Timothy Winchester upstairs, waiting to go over all of the arrangements. He's the owner of the traveling freak show that the twins were part of and they need to keep moving in order to make all of their contracted stops. They need the funeral to happen by tomorrow morning at the latest. You know Carnies, it's always about the next show." Taking one last look at the dead twins, James exited the room and left Chester to start the preservation process.

"Carnies are a fiercely loyal bunch. All we have is each other," stated a duo of voices from behind him. When Chester turned around, he saw the women sitting up, clasping modesty cloths to their chests.

"Your father's wrong if he thinks all our friend's care about is getting to the next town. We've always had a strict pact in the event any of us dies." The synchronized voices were unnerving and Chester just stared at the two women, not quite sure what to say. He opened his mouth to speak but no words came out. Instead, he just continued to stare at them.

"Don't worry, we're used to people staring at us," the conjoined twins stated in their creepy synchronization. "Do you happen to know who we are?"

"No clue," Chester said honestly.

"We're Holly and Rose: The Amazing Gideon Sisters," they answered simultaneously, smiling at something that Chester was acutely unaware of. "Listen, we have a favor to ask you."

"What is it?"

"Separate us."

"W…what?"

"We've been joined at the hip for thirty-seven years. We'd like to experience what it feels like to be apart."

"Ummm… But you share a leg…" Chester commented. He had absolutely no intention of separating them. How could he ever explain that to his father? It wasn't like James wouldn't notice, and when he did, he'd definitely disapprove.

Rose and Holly must have seen the answer written plainly on Chester's face. Scooting themselves over to the edge of the table, they hung their three legs over the side for a moment before hopping to the floor. They landed somewhat unsteadily, looking for a moment like they might fall over. Once they had steadied themselves, they began to search the room.

Guessing their intent was to perform the separation themselves, Chester moved in front of the drawers containing the knives and saws, thinking that by standing in front of them, he would deter the twins. But his movement had the opposite effect, the action like a beacon to them. They honed in on him and the drawers, strongly pushing him aside in the quest, opening each one until they found the tools they desired. As each of them withdrew their hands from the drawer, bone saws of different sizes came with them. They turned to look at Chester with grim determination written across their faces.

"Are you sure you won't help us?"

Chester just stared wide-eyed at them, aghast at what they were prepared to do to each other.

"Do you want to do it?" one asked the other. Her hand shook slightly in her excitement and apprehension of the coming moment.

"Yes, I'll do it. You can't even draw a straight line," the other replied, a funny look overshadowing her face.

Chester watched in horror as one twin placed her saw at the junction where their hips met and started to move it back and forth. There was more blood than Chester expected, but nothing stopped him from watching the scene unfold before him. Somewhere in the back of his mind, his thoughts raced back and forth, furiously trying to work out what he was going to tell his father. Not that James was going to understand or accept any explanation that Chester came up with, of course.

The twin with the saw finished and stepped away. With her support gone, the other twin fell to the floor.

"Rose, what did you do?" Holly screamed from the floor. "You were supposed to cut evenly down the middle!"

When Rose didn't answer her sister, the shouting started. "You bitch! You kept the leg all for yourself, you selfish troll! I can't believe you'd do this to me. What am I supposed to do now?"

Chester heard the telltale creak of the third stair and knew his father was about to be extremely angry. As James burst into the room, he stopped short, surveying the scene before him.

Both Holly and Rose were on the floor, a bloody saw lying between them. Turning to look at Chester, James couldn't even form a question. Instead, he grabbed his chest, pain contorting his face. He was dead before he hit the mint green tile.

Within a second he was back up on his feet, looking at his son with new eyes.

"I tried to tell you, Dad. I tried to tell you that they're not completely dead."

James merely stared at Chester, the twins, and himself, unable to believe what was happening.

Chester smiled, satisfied that for the first time in his life, someone in his family actually believed him.

THE MOTHER OF ZOMBIES

GRETCHEN ELHASSANI

It's late evening as I write this, in the lull after one of their feedings. I've learned their cycles and when it's safe to move around, to clean up. No one can know of the horror that goes on in this house. It wasn't always this way; I can remember clearly when we were all a happy, normal family.

I'm a mom. My children were in first grade and third grade. I have a six-year-old and an eight-year-old—both boys. Our house is full of toy trucks and sports equipment, trading cards, action figures, superhero action figures and comic books. Their rooms are overflowing with toys that I'd bought for them in many moments of weakness. I know I'm trying to make up for the incompleteness of their lives, as if buying plastic junk will ever make up for being a single parent. Their father ran off with another woman, dare I say, a thinner woman, about three years ago. I don't know how long they were dating before they finally told me. I had no idea it was happening, and it uprooted my world. All that energy I'd put into the marriage, into staying on top of the household chores, picking up the kids, cooking dinners, hand-making Father's Day gifts; none of it meant anything to him. He wanted beautiful and sexy, and I was stressed-out and spit-up-on in faded jeans.

I was angry for a long time.

He moved out of the house and in with her. They have visitation of the children one night per week and one weekend a month, but they rarely use it. Seems they would rather be necking in their hot tub rather than watching ninja shows and cleaning up cereal spills on Saturday mornings. I don't care, or that's what I used to tell myself, because my beautiful children are my life.

I got a job as a secretary at a local elementary school. It's not the school my children go to, but it's in the same district so we have the same holidays off, and it works out well. Or should I say, it *worked* out well. My six-year-old was a little behind on his reading, so I purchased a massive amount of little phonics books, and we were reading them every night, until about a month ago.

That's when something horrible happened to my little angel, my first born son, at a birthday party. I had taken the boys to buy presents at the local shopping mall. They each chose a deck of trading cards for the lucky birthday boy, and we wrapped as we sat inside the car before driving over to the party.

It was at one of those play places that features bouncy castles and pizza for groups of ten to twenty energetic young partygoers. I was sitting with the rest of the mothers, trying to talk about light subjects like school and yoga, trying not to let on that I was divorced. Then, from across the room, I heard my first born scream.

I got up from my seat and raced over to a massive moon bounce that was built like a fortress, with a series of inflatable posts standing guard at the entrance. I could hear my child screaming from within the contraption, so I pushed my way through.

The floor of the moon bounce rippled gently beneath my feet, as I climbed through a tunnel, up a faux rock wall, and slid down an inflatable slide into the bouncing arena. There I found my son, fighting with another small boy.

I bounced across the floor to pull the two apart, horrified by the violent light in the other boy's eyes. "Where's your mother?" I demanded. The child didn't speak, but glared at me with a hatred I'd never seen in anyone so young.

"Come on." I gathered my son to my chest, leading him sobbing out through the plastic maze. Once our feet touched solid ground, I turned around to look at him.

"Mom, he bit me." Adam cried, tears staining his little cheeks.

"Where? Let me see?" I demanded, running my hands across his shoulders.

"Here." Adam pointed to his right arm, where a splotch of red was beginning to show beneath the fabric of his shirt.

I pulled up the shirtsleeve carefully, determined not to hurt him anymore. Glowing against his skin was a round set of teeth marks, thick with red blood. I couldn't believe any child could bite so hard! Furious, I stormed over to the group of moms, frantic to know who had brought the offending child.

"Someone bit my son!" I cried, holding Adam's arm out as proof as I dragged him behind me.

"Who?" one of the moms gasped.

"I don't know; some child in there." I pointed back to the monstrous castle.

"All right, everybody out!" The staff of the party place had heard the outcry and came to the rescue, demanding every child line up for inspection. I found my six-year-old, unharmed, playing on a different moon bounce. As the children assembled, it was clear they were all disappointed to be interrupted in their play. The evil child with the hatred in his eyes didn't emerge, and the mothers looked to me for clarification.

"He was in there." I pointed to the castle, sending one of the teenaged staff—a girl of sixteen—into the maze to hunt for the boy.

She came out empty handed. "I don't see anyone in there, ma'am."

"He was in there, I swear." I started to lose my cool, now concerned about getting the bleeding to stop on Adam's arm. "I'm going to take my son to the hospital."

"I'm sorry." The host of the party approached me as I hunted out my boys' shoes and jackets from the locker room. She wore a look of concern on her face.

"Someone else is going to get hurt." I promised her. "Because that little boy, he…" I didn't know how to describe it, the way the child had attacked my son. I shook my head. "Adam, Charlie, put your shoes on."

"Mom, I don't want to go," Charlie whined.

"Charlie, Adam was bitten. He's bleeding. We have to take him to the hospital and have his arm looked at," I responded, less than patiently.

"Oh, man." The little boy scuffed his foot, wasted time getting his shoes on, and made a miserable show of making me look like the worst mom in the world. I hated when he did that.

I wrapped my jacket around Adam's arm, and drove him to the hospital. It took six hours from when we checked in, until we were released. He saw three doctors, all of whom were very friendly, and gently examined the bite and took notes. A nurse came to clean the wound, and we were given a prescription for antibiotics, just in case the attacking child had some kind of disease. They gave Adam some ibuprofen for the pain, bandaged his arm, and sent us on our way with a print-out of warning signs to look for. Nowhere in that handout did it mention the horrible reality that actually came to pass.

Adam was fine for two days: eating, sleeping, playing, watching TV, everything he did was normal. We took off the bandage and washed it once per day, applying antibiotic ointment and a new bandage each night before bed. On the third day, he stopped eating. That was when I saw a piece on my social network feed that said they were quarantining people who had been bitten by other people.

Quarantine?

Now that's a nasty word for an eight-year-old. No one was going to quarantine my boy. Take him away from home? Lock him up with other people who had been bitten? What was going on? I had no idea, but I kept my son home from school that day.

The next morning it was hard to wake Adam up, and I had a panic attack, thinking that something from the print-out the doctors gave me was coming true.

When he did finally come around, he was groggy and unfocused. I called in sick from work and kept Charlie home, too. I set Charlie up with some cereal in front of the television, and went back to check on Adam.

I found Adam standing in his room, dressed in his pajamas, and staring at the wall.

"Sweetheart?" I said, coming around to place a hand on his shoulder.

There was no reaction.

"Sweetheart, I'm scared. Are you okay?" I looked down at the bandage and imagined all the sick, horrible things that could be happening to him. I never imagined this could ever happen. "Sweetheart, let's get dressed."

He turned on me with a rage in his eyes that reminded me of the little boy in the bouncy castle. My little angel pounced on me, wrapping strong hands around my forearms and pressing his greedy mouth to my stomach. I fell back against the bed, twisting myself free to hold him at arm's length. He thrashed his head, spitting and growling and clawing his way towards me.

"Charlie!" I cried. "Charlie, come help me!"

Charlie ran into the room, his little feet pattering swiftly on the hallway floor. "Mom?" he called, concerned.

"Charlie, get me some rope or something!" I screamed, desperate to subdue Adam without hurting him. He was crazy, enraged, like some possessed animal.

Charlie took one look at both of us and stepped into the room, not understanding what was happening.

"Charlie, no." I said quietly, foreseeing the situation a sheer instant before it happened.

Adam took one look at Charlie, younger, smaller, less able to fight him than me. He let me go and charged towards Charlie, chasing him out into the living room. Charlie screamed, dashing his way through the house, to the kitchen, where he boxed himself between the refrigerator and the stove.

"Mom!" Charlie cried. "Help me!"

I ran after them, tackling Adam to the kitchen floor, but not before he had wrapped his arms around Charlie and bitten down, hard, on Charlie's left forearm. Charlie screamed in pain and terror, wiggling out from under Adam's teeth as I pinned my oldest son to the floor. Adam twisted and spat, his mouth red with Charlie's blood. It took all my strength to keep him down, mounted to the floor. I looked around, wild and sick, trying to figure out what to do next.

I knew Charlie was traumatized, bleeding and in pain. I wanted to go to him, but had no choice but to ask for his help. "Charlie, I need you to go into the basement and find some rope."

"Mom, I'm bleeding! Adam bit me!" Charlie screamed, holding out his thin arm for scrutiny. "Adam *bit* me!"

"Go, sweetheart!" I yelled, already feeling my arms weaken from the thrashing Adam was giving them.

Charlie tiptoed around us both, scurrying into the basement. I heard his feet on the stairs five minutes later, his voice sobbing, "Mom, I can't find any rope."

"Look near Daddy's tool box." I called back, closing my eyes to find the strength to hold on to Adam. Charlie returned with the rope two minutes later, and I told him to place it on the floor. "Okay, now go into your room, close the door and don't come out until I say it's okay."

"But my arm?"

"Get a towel from the bathroom. I'll be there in a minute to help you with it."

Charlie looked down at his brother, or at the *creature* that his brother had become. He nodded with all his six years of wisdom, and hurried off to lock himself away. I let up from Adam and lunged for the rope.

In an instant, he was on me, trying to bite. I knocked him away, God forgive me, but I hit my child. When he was down, I pinned his arms behind him and wrapped them firm with the rope. Using up all of my remaining strength, I carried him down the stairs and tied him to a set of metal shelves that were bolted to the wall. Gasping for air, and sick with the thought of this also happening to Charlie, I climbed the steps again to face my youngest.

Charlie was waiting in his room, hiding in the corner. I knocked softly, calling out through the door, even as my voice hiccupped in despair. "Charlie, it's Mommy."

"Mommy?" Charlie whispered, coming to the bedroom door. He let me in, holding his wounded arm, his big eyes wide and wet. "Why did Adam bite me?"

"I don't know, sweetheart." I whispered, gathering him to my chest. We held each other for a long time, then went to the bathroom to clean and dress Charlie's wound.

"What's going to happen to me now?" Charlie asked, the terror of the morning still fresh.

"Nothing, sweetpea," I reassured him. "You're going to be fine."

"What's going to happen to Adam?"

"You let me worry about Adam," I said.

"Is he mad at me?"

"Oh no, honey, he's not mad at you. He's just…" I had no way to describe it, no understanding of the events that made any sense. All I knew is that I couldn't take my boys to the hospital again, or they would be taken away from me and quarantined.

Two days was all the time I had between when Adam was bitten, and when he turned. Two days was all I had left with Charlie.

I took him out to do all the fun things he loved to do, like go to the Pizza Arcade, play on the playground, shop for toys. He did it all with a heavy heart, his beautiful brown eyes deep pools of fear and worry. He knew what was happening. He slept with me both nights, with buckets of popcorn in front of the television. I gave him everything his little heart desired, and then tied him up and put him in the basement with his brother.

A day after Charlie turned, I noticed Adam getting weak. He no longer thrashed against his bindings or tried to lunge for me when I came close. I cooked them chicken nuggets, their favorite, and tried to get them to eat, but Charlie only wanted a piece of my flesh, and Adam couldn't summon interest in anything anymore, as he was so weak.

I couldn't let them die. Without eating, they would starve to death. It was clear from their behavior what they wanted to eat, but I couldn't offer myself, not without risking all our lives.

My first victim was the plumber. I called to say there was some gunk coming up in the basement drain, and could someone come over right away to fix it. The receptionist said she would see how soon someone was available, and asked if I was going to be at the house. I said yes, and politely waited while she checked schedules. She said someone could come over sometime between 3-5 p.m. I scheduled the service and then hung up.

For the rest of the day, I went around cleaning the house, especially the boys' rooms. I put every toy back in its toy bin, put clean sheets on the beds, mopped the floors, and even cleaned out the closets. I picked out some new clothes for them to wear, and folded them neatly on the kitchen table. I made myself something to eat for later, did some vacuuming, cleaned the bathroom, and made my bed. When three o'clock came around and the plumber still hadn't arrived, I think part of me was almost relieved. But I had brought my children into the world, raised them. I was responsible for their survival, and if, forgive me, their survival meant doing what I was about to do, then so be it.

The doorbell rang.

I brushed my hair out with my hand and stood up to answer it. Trying to affect my least, *'I'm about to feed you to my zombie children in the basement'* attitude, I led the plumber to the kitchen and offered him a cup of coffee.

"No thank you, ma'am." He nodded curtly. "So, where's the problem?"

"You're sure you don't want a cup of coffee?" I tried again, trying to stall his painful death.

"No, ma'am, I'm fine." He had no idea what I was talking about.

"Okay." I picked up a pair of scissors from the kitchen counter, and hid them behind my back, then directed the man to the basement, where I said the laundry sink was.

He looked at me trustingly, then followed me down to the basement without a thought in the world of what might be waiting for him. The sink was at one end, and the metal shelves my children were tied to were at the other end, and now a tall divider had been placed before them to hide them from view. So it was a simple task to direct the plumber towards the sink, while sneaking off to untie my children while his back was turned.

The man was bent over the basin, searching in vain for this mysterious gunk I'd called about. I watched as Charlie took off across the floor, plowing into the poor man from behind.

"What the hell?" the plumber shrieked, and whirled around to disentangle a monstrous six-year-old from his leg. He stumbled back, as if to kick Charlie away, when I grabbed a shovel from the corner. I picked up the makeshift weapon, and while he was distracted with Charlie, I hit him over the head.

The man bowed towards the floor, reaching up to cradle his head in his hands. Charlie leapt on him with a rabid feeding frenzy, tearing through the man's windpipe. I put the shovel down and went over to Adam, who was untied but languishing beside the shelves. I helped him up gently, urging him forward with a mother's hand. I led him over to the man, where Charlie had the plumber down on the floor, digging thick chunks of meat out from gnawed holes in the clothing. Adam fell to his knees and dug in, the wicked light flashing on in his eyes as he filled himself with bloody meat.

I watched my two children eat their fill, then went back upstairs to lock the door.

When I returned, I stood over them and watched. I let my head drop, tears hovering at the corners of my eyes. My beautiful children. My reason for living.

I waited until evening, then crept downstairs to clean up after the boys, just as I always have. They were nowhere to be seen, but I knew they were around because I hadn't seen them come out. The plumber was right where I'd left him, though considerably smaller than when he'd entered. It wasn't difficult to lift what was left of him, and scrape it into garbage bags, then carry it all upstairs. I found his keys in a gnawed-off pocket of his pants and used them to start up his truck. I put the bags of gore into the back of the truck, and drove it down to a park by the river, about two miles away from my house. I buried the bags and left the truck with the keys in the ignition, then walked home. Before I left, I made sure to try and wipe down as many places as I thought I'd touched inside the truck—just in case. I'd seen enough crime shows on TV to at least try not to get caught.

That night in my house, with my boys in the basement, was the loneliest night of my life. I took a shower to clean off all the remnants of the plumber. Then I took the boys' clean clothes into the basement. I found Charlie, sleeping or unconscious, near the water heater. I got him out of his blood-soaked pants, and pulled the damp shirt over his head. The clean clothes went on as if he were my overgrown baby, asleep in his cradle, as I maneuvered limp limbs through the arm holes of the shirt.

I found Adam near the work bench, and dressing him was more difficult because of his age. When I finished, I now had two clean, well-fed boys, who just happened to be sleeping on the floor in the basement, instead of in their rooms upstairs. That's what I told myself, so I could live through it.

I disposed of their dirty clothes, locked the basement door, and poured myself glass after glass of wine until I passed out at the kitchen table.

When Adam was a baby, and I was exhausted from so many sleepless nights that one time I had to put him in his crib and let him cry to get him to take a nap. I sat outside his door for twenty minutes, listening to him scream, wanting to go to him, but knowing he was tired and needed to wind himself down. It was torture, pure and simple.

The first night I fed my undead boys was like that, knowing that they had to stay in the basement, though I wanted to go to them and hug them tight.

But there would be no more hugs for my children.

After that first feeding, I learned more about what my boys had become. I learned that they needed to eat about every three days to stay 'healthy.'

In the beginning, I called more plumbers, as that ruse had worked quite well. In all, I dialed three plumbing shops before I got scared that someone would catch on to what I was doing.

After that, I tried ordering pizza, then making up an excuse about how I was scared to go in the basement, and could they help me get the lights back on.

I ordered two pizza delivery men that way, then parked their cars in a bad part of town with the keys in the ignition and the doors unlocked, knowing the vehicles would be stolen.

I got a bible salesman who conveniently came to our door, to 'take a look at my sick children.' Then I grabbed my neighbor, which I really shouldn't have done, because that was striking way too close to home. But I was desperate and running out of options.

The boys were hungry again last night, and there was one last person I knew I could call. He'd left us years ago, without so much as an explanation as to why.

He hadn't even called once in the past month, since the boys turned and I'd been greedily feeding them every pound of flesh I could find.

I called their father, my ex-husband. I was determined to find a lie that would get the man over to my house and into the basement.

"Hello, James." It was hard to find anything but anger where he was concerned.

"Hi, Katherine," he responded, more at ease than I was. "How are the boys?"

"That's what I wanted to talk to you about." I scoured my mind for a suitable lie, one that would entice him to come to our rescue, and not dump the whole problem back in my lap. "Adam has a school project where he has to repair a bike."

"Repair a bike?" James loved repairing bikes, but couldn't understand how that was a child's project.

"They're working on it for science class; it's like a small motor or something."

"It's not a small motor," James corrected me. Stupid me.

"Anyway," I rushed on, "I've been trying to help him, and the project is due tomorrow, and I know you're busy, but he could really use your help."

James sighed. "Okay. I'll come after work."

"Great!" I cheered. "I'll cook you something for dinner."

"Don't do that." He shot me down. "I'm just helping Adam with his bike project, then I'm leaving."

"Charlie will love to see you, too." I reminded him.

"How's Charlie doing with his reading?" James asked, remembering something about his son.

"You can ask him yourself when you see him," I said.

"It will be good to see them," James lied.

"Yes it will. Thank you for coming," I put in, lest he forget I was grateful for his assistance.

Oh yes, he would see his boys. I cooked dinner just to annoy him, just to see his face when he walked in the door, with the pots steaming on the stove, after he'd just told me not to.

Was I warming up to my two monsters in the basement?

Was I actually enjoying the thought that they were about to munch on my arch nemesis?

Perhaps.

I was nearly giggling with delight by the time he dropped by.

As I predicted, his mood was sour when he saw dinner on the stove. "I told you not to cook."

"Oh," I pretended innocence, "it's just for me and the boys. You can stay if you want to."

"No. I have plans." He wasn't fooled, and suspected I'd done it just to annoy him. "Where are the boys?" he asked.

"They're in the basement, working on the bike," I answered happily.

Without another word to me, he turned, opened the basement door, and stomped down the steps. I closed the door behind him, locked it, and went back to cooking my meal.

It would be a lot for one person to eat, but the look on his face was so worth it. I even chuckled when I heard him scream.

FROST BITE

MARILYN SIMPSON

"Come on, Jules, you can make it." David had to yell to be heard over the blowing winds. He grabbed Jules' hand and pulled his girlfriend over a log that had fallen across the almost-hidden road. Snow was blasting them to the point where they could just follow the outlines of the road as it wound through the towering pines.

As darkness fell, the world dissolved into different shades of whirling grays. Just putting one foot in front of the other took all David's strength and he could only wonder how Jules was able to keep moving, but stopping would mean their deaths, for there was no way they could ride out the storm without shelter.

They had traveled north into Canada to escape the zombie hordes that were growing within the United States, but it wouldn't do them any good if they froze to death.

"I'm not sure if I can make it," Jules panted, while resting her hands on her knees. "Should we even be going this way? Why would the gas stations be shut down? I thought the cold was keeping Canada safe? And where is everyone?"

"I'm not sure, angel, but if everyone is gone that might be a good thing. Then we could take over the first house we find." He avoided her eyes as he spoke. "This road has to lead somewhere, and even if it is just someone's summer cabin, hopefully we can find some food and get out of this cold."

Minutes seemed to feel like hours as Jules and David struggled to maintain their pace, each eager to find some sort of refuge from the cold. David knew Jules was finding it hard to keep it together. He tried to reassure her best as he could, but he couldn't help but wonder if their luck had finally run out.

They reached the end of the desolate road and turned to walk along a snow-covered pathway. After more trudging through the deep snow, they saw a light shining from a building in the distance. Jules looked at David with eyes mixed with relief and uncertainty.

As they started their hike up the steep hill, they suddenly heard a woman screaming. Jules stopped and it went silent. She listened. Then a roar of winds eclipsed the screaming. After giving her what he hoped was a reassuring look, David took Jules by the hand and led her toward the light.

"Why are we going someplace where we just heard a scream?" she asked, her whole body convulsing in a shiver that might not have been due to the cold. For a moment, only the crunching of the snow and the driving winds answered her.

"I can think of several reasons, David said. 'The first is that we'll die out here anyway. Another is there could be people there that could use our help. Also, we should keep it in mind, and forgive my gloomy thoughts, but if they're already dead, and the place is safe, we might be able to claim it for ourselves."

"That's horrible."

"Yeah, sorry, I'm just so cold. But what I really hope is that we don't get shot by someone mistaking us for a couple of zombies," he said.

Jules gripped his hand tighter as they drew near to what looked like a backwoods lodge of some kind.

"This looks too big to be someone's house," he said.

"Unless they're super rich," she added.

Drawing nearer, they saw a crescent driveway under a rustic overhang. Two pillars curved from ancient trees, which were wider than David could fit his arms around, supported overhang. Past this was a set of wooded doors. A dim light could be seen through a curtained window; no further sounds were heard.

David saw a silhouette of someone pacing inside when he peered through the window. "I sure hope whoever lives here is friendly," he whispered, while walking closer to the door. "I can't see anyone now."

"Do you think this is a good idea?" Jules asked. "What if they're waiting for us?"

Before David could answer, the front door slowly opened, to reveal an old lady standing before them. The old woman's frail figure was bent forward and twisted. Her bony hands clasped the heavy door as she lifted her sickly head to greet them.

"What can I do for you?"

They were surprised at how pleasant and young her voice sounded.

Jules released a breath she didn't know she was holding. "We were hoping you might have a room we could rent for the night."

The old lady smiled and gestured them inside. "I'm sure I do."

Inside the dim house, a large hound greeted them. David hated dogs and tried his best to deter it, but failed, and the dirty hound was all over him with its drool and stench. As David and Jules looked around, they saw that everything looked filthy and in disarray.

"This is a little weird," she whispered. "But at least we're out of the cold."

Putting his head close to Jules' ear, David said. "It seems strange she hasn't mentioned the undead plague or anything about it. She's just acting like everything's normal and people wander in on foot in the middle of a blizzard all the time."

Turning toward the old woman, he continued in a louder voice, "It's very quiet here. Is it always like this?" he asked, staring into the woman's grayish eyes.

"No," she replied, but failed to say more.

Suddenly they heard a sound of heavy feet stumbling down the stairs. Jules moved toward David and grabbed his hand.

"No need to worry," the old lady smirked. "You're safe here. They're heading out into the night."

David didn't have to ask who *they* were. He already knew.

"What the hell?" he cried, grabbing Jules' arm. "We need to get outta here!"

"Oh, don't be alarmed, young man. Everything is fine," the old woman said.

"Everything's fine?" he gasped, as the first tattered corpse came into view. "They're going to be all over us. We have to…"

"You hush up. These *walkers* are more harmless than a new-born kitten."

Jules was stunned and David just stood there.

The couple looked at each other with wide eyes. The zombies were ignoring them and instead exited out a side door. There were about thirty in all. Their flesh was a greenish black from rot and they all wore faded, torn clothing, but there was one other odd thing about them. Each zombie looked as though they were wearing a new pair of boots.

"Why aren't they attacking us?" Jules found the courage to ask.

"Allow me to answer that question," a voice called from the top of the stairs. A man came down the steps in no great haste. He wore a stained lab coat, which might have been white a year ago, over a maroon smoking jacket. His gray hair was combed and he smoothed his fingers over his thin moustache before saying, "I'm Professor Hunter, as well as your host." His shifty eyes focused on

Jules and carefully watched her every move. David saw this unsettled her.

"So, are you going to answer the question?" David asked. "And we thought we heard a scream earlier. Can you explain that?"

"Patience, young man," Prof. Hunter smirked as he led them into another room. Inside his office, the room was so small there was barely enough space for his old antique desk and chair. Hunter sat down and rubbed his hands together, while David and Jules stood before him.

"I have something that may interest you, David."

"How did you know my name?"

Prof. Hunter slowly raised himself. "Remember Dr. Edwards?" He reached under his desk, removed a large brown box, and placed it on the desk. "In here is what you've been looking for."

Jules frowned, while David wiped the sweat from his brow and scanned the box. His trembling hand slowly reached out.

"Damn." David looks into Prof. Hunter's eyes, "Damn you." Lurching to his feet, he hovered for a moment, then hurried out of the room. After one last look at Prof. Hunter and his odd box, Jules ran after David.

As if throwing young couples into chaos was a daily occurrence, Prof. Hunter smiled and lit a cigarette. After taking a long puff off smoke, he leaned back and patiently waited.

His fingers gently thrummed the wooden box

He knew they would return.

Jules grabbed David's arm before he could dash off into the growing blizzard, the door already open, the cold air pouring in. "What're you doing? Stop!" She had to scream to be heard over the whipping wind. "We can't go out into this storm. We'd be dead before we made it a mile, even without the zombies."

Shaking his head, he gazed out into the storm while the snow fell into the oversized porch.

"David, what's going on? You have to tell me!"

Grabbing her by both arms and looking into her eyes, he said, "Jules, I haven't been completely honest with you. Remember that Dr. Edwards I told you about?" She nodded. "Well, he was one of the first people to take this plague seriously, and as soon as the dead started walking, he began experiments on them. Where others thought we could contain the problem, he knew better and told me about this remote location where a former coworker of his was holed up. His plan from the very beginning was to design a way to control the zombies. He thought that if we could somehow make them attack each other and hunt down their own kind, it would be the only way we could survive this mess. Apparently, his idea worked."

"So what's the problem and what was in that box?"

"The problem is that the only way we can control the zombies is by injecting them with the cerebellum of living people." Jules gasped and it was his turn to nod. "So yes, it can work, but is it worth the price? For every human brain that has to be destroyed, every human killed in the process, we might be able to control eight or ten zombies. Some might think it's worth it."

"What, how!"

"Well, the zombies would never tire, would never stop. Other zombies wouldn't see them as a threat and could do little to hurt them. Where ten strong men might have to be fed and housed, ten enslaved zombies could live forever in some spare room and protect an area at little cost."

"Also, think about it, if a soldier gets bit and infected, he soon dies and switches sides. The enslaved zombies could be sent out to kill their own kind day and night for weeks on end."

"But to kill people… There are already so few of us left."

"I know, my dear, and that's why you're so precious." Prof. Hunter's voice lifted above the winds and Jules and David stiffened in fear. Then they heard the moaning.

The young couple had been so distracted by their conversation and the storm, they didn't see that the zombies had returned and were reaching out to them with decayed hands. David tried to struggle, to run with Jules, but there were simply too many.

As David tried to fight off the undead, he wasn't unaware that the professor had moved up behind him, that is until the man lifted up the rifle he was carrying and struck David on the head with the butt.

Immediately, David collapsed to the snow-covered ground, Jules screams echoing in his ears before he lost consciousness.

David felt a cold hand grip his arm tightly. He quickly sat up as an angelic-looking woman let go of her grasp. He looked into her dark blue eyes. She seemed so beautiful. He scanned the old barn he now found himself in. A few chickens scampered by. He tried to stand, but a sudden pain engulfed him and forced him to stop. The dark-haired woman picked herself up, flicked some straw out of her messy hair, and rubbed her tiny hands against her dirty white dress, as she continued to stare at him with her wide eyes.

"Who are you? What the hell am I doing here?" David demanded.

The woman didn't reply.

David touched the back of his head and grimaced. "Did the zombies bring me here?"

Again the woman said nothing.

"I have to find Jules. Do you know where she is?"

The woman started to kick her bare feet in the dirty straw. David stood up again, and this time didn't feel faint. He approached the woman. "Answer me. What's going on? Where am I?" He tried a different approach. "Are you okay? Did that bastard Hunter do something to hurt you?"

Again the woman acted more like a distracted child than someone in her twenties. Slowly, David approached the young woman. There was a red scar at the side of her temple. "He's been experimenting on you hasn't he? That bastard has taken out parts of your brain!"

She hummed an odd, lilting melody and acted like he wasn't there. A shiver ran up his spine. Then a noise was heard from outside and the barn door opened.

"Perfect. He's awake. David, I think it's time," Prof. Hunter said as he stood in the opening.

"Time for what?" David snarled. As Hunter walked in, David's eyes grew wider when he saw four zombies following the man.

"Must you be so melodramatic, David? I think you already know."

"How could you justify these actions? How could even a hundred trained zombies be equal to one living, breathing man?"

Hunter sighed. "Haven't you already gone over this with your lovely girlfriend, David? The zombies I create will never tire, never need to be fed, and now more importantly, not be bothered with whatever liberties I take with young Jules. Little Carrie here has proved to be a fun toy, but there's something about touching a hollow-minded woman... Well, I still find unnerving."

"You murdering bastard! What have you done to Jules?"

"Oh nothing yet, but I'm looking forward to many enjoyable things," he laughed. "Don't you see? I'll soon be the zombie king in control of these lands and any good king needs a queen. And I'd prefer one that isn't slowly rotting." He looked over at Carrie, "Or acts like a child."

Looking around, David's eyes landed on a long garden hoe and he snatched it up.

"Oh please, don't make a mess, will you? My zombies are much stronger than you. You certainly have no chance here."

"Oh really?" David said, flashing his teeth, right before he knocked an oil lantern onto the straw covering the floor. Carrie stumbled away from the fire, letting out a low moan, while the zombies backed away groaning.

Prof. Hunter let loose a stream of curses followed by, "You fool, you'll ruin everything!"

"That's the plan."

Prof. Hunter removed his coat and, as he dashed over to stop the flames from spreading, David saw his chance to escape. While he fled, David swung the hoe to either side, forcing two zombies to stumble and fall. After he ran out into the night, he could hear Prof. Hunter scream, "Go after him, you idiots!"

David knew they would catch him soon. He had to return to the house and find Jules before they did.

When he reached the house, he found that the door had been left open. As he moved through the door, he thought he heard Jules' voice.

Could she be upstairs? He wondered. Without a second thought, he quickly made his way up the dark narrow staircase. When he reached the top, he was surprised to see Prof. Hunter waiting for him.

Prof. Hunter's sinister grin chilled David to the core. As he stood before the man, something caught his eye. "How did you beat me up here?"

"You can't best me within my own house, you fool. There are other ways to get in here. I have my zombies with me, too!" he yelled, but David was barely paying attention, for his eyes had spotted a fire poker that sat outside of a second floor fireplace.

He raced for it. It filled his hand and he turned around only to find that Prof. Hunter had a weapon of his own, and the rifle certainly looked more dangerous than his meager fire poker.

"Ah, not much of a fight considering I have a gun, but I never did like to play fair." Between Prof. Hunter's boasts, the groaning of the zombies entering below could be heard.

"What have you done with Jules? Tell me!"

"I've told you, she won't be harmed," he grinned wickedly. "At least not much. But you on the other hand, I can't make the same promise. Now, let's be a good boy and give up, hmm? No matter what you try, you can't win."

David tossed the fire poker at Prof. Hunter in response. Prof. Hunter blocked it quickly, but the sharp point took him in the cheek, drawing blood. "You little worm, I'll make your ending slow for that!"

David turned and ran. His only hope was that he might be running the right way. He rushed by closed doors as he ran, dreading the thought that each of them could be the one that held his Jules.

"You fool," Prof. Hunter's voice echoed after him. "Where do you hope to run to?"

David turned the corner to find half a dozen zombies lumbering his way.

"Shit!" he swore through clenched teeth and raced into a random room and quickly locked the door behind him.

The zombies banged on the walls and paced outside the door. David ran over to a window. He was up on the second floor, but he didn't have much choice. He opened the window and climbed out onto the ledge, then carefully made his way down to the roof that covered the front porch.

Dropping to his stomach, David let his legs hang over the side of the porch roof and prepared to drop down to the ground. That was when he felt someone firmly grasp his right leg, the fingers digging into his flesh. David closed his eyes and cried out in pain. Then he moved his head to look. It was Prof. Hunter, who was laughing.

"Damn you! Let go of me!" David shouted and struggled to break free. Prof. Hunter grabbed David with both hands and pulled him off the roof. David tumbled off, landing on his back, the wind knocked from him.

"You can't escape me, David. Why do you even try?" His evil laugh grew louder.

David tried to stand, but Prof. Hunter pushed him back down onto the porch. David could hear the zombies and all he could do was wait. As they came out, Jules was with them.

"Jules, oh thank God," David said, pleased to see she was still alive, but when he saw she was holding the wooden box in her hand, a cold chill ran through him.

"Open the box, my dear," Prof. Hunter said.

"No." David pleaded. "No, don't do this!"

She looked at David and then Prof. Hunter, who nodded and said, "You know you have to, my dear."

Before David could move to stop her, Jules opened the box. She stared for a good three seconds at its contents, and then, after uttering a quick shriek, dropped the box. It crashed to the ground and something the size of a fist bounced out of it.

David, who had stood up, now sank to his knees in defeat.

"It's a human heart," Jules said, growing pale. "What does this have to do with anything?"

Prof. Hunter's voice grew soft. "When you first arrived, I thought you to be just random travelers, but very quickly I recognized that David was Dr. Edwards pet. A happy coincidence if I do say so myself."

"His pet?" Jules said. Wide-eyed and alarmed, she took a step away from them.

"Yes, he was…an experiment. You see, my dear, that isn't any random heart that lies at your feet. It's David's heart."

Tears began to roll down her cheeks. "Wait, I…I don't understand."

"Dr. Edwards and I were experimenting with reanimation. David had an accident while he was assisting us. One of our other…*projects* escaped and stabbed an IV pole through David's chest. He would have surely died, but Dr. Edwards administered his new formula quickly and David became the first man to live without a heart, or should I say, the first walking corpse."

David sunk down lower, his head hanging limply while he stared at the heart.

"But… but David isn't dead. His body is warm. He's breathing. I've touched him."

"Correct, dear, and if I chopped off his arm he would scream and bleed, at least some. He's what Dr. Edwards and I had hoped for, had worked so diligently for, but then Edwards got greedy. He used the formula on someone fully dead. The results were less pleasant. In fact, not only did it cost Edwards his life, but it also cost humanity its civilization. You see it was Edwards who inadvertently started the undead plague."

"I…I don't believe it."

"It's true, Jules," David said without looking up.

Prof. Hunter gave Jules a pitying smile. "I suppose you just thought this was a random trip, and you were lucky to find someone like David who could help you get somewhere safe, but this isn't true, is it, David?"

David just groaned.

"You see, my dear, your new boyfriend is looking for something."

David finally looked up; his face was clammy and white. "Don't, please."

Prof. Hunter laughed. "She already knows you have no heart, what else matters now? Do you have any left or did you already run out?"

David didn't answer.

"What're you talking about?" Jules looked at David. She looked like she wanted to comfort him, but now she wasn't so sure.

"You see, my dear, David needs an injection of the formula to stay…alive. I'm sure he was hoping I had some, for I'm the only person that would."

"Well, do you?" David stared at Hunter, waiting for the answer.

"Oh, I might have some. The question is: what are you going to do for me?"

"What do you want?" David growled.

David slowly opened his eyes to find himself chained to a bed. He was bound so tight that he could barely move. He tried to remember what happened, but all he could picture was Prof. Hunter's piercing eyes staring at him.

David looked around at the dirty, off-white walls. There was a tiny window that was letting in some light and he heard the sound of birds chirping outside.

Birds? How long have I been here? And what does that bastard want to do with me now? He wondered.

He shouted for someone to help him, but was only greeted with silence. The minutes stretched to hours and he wondered if he was truly all alone. Could Prof. Hunter have lost control of his undead?

Then he heard a key turning in the lock on the door.

"Jules?" he said as she entered.

She didn't respond.

"Thank God it's you," he said anxiously. "Untie me, quick, before Hunter comes back." As he stared at her, he realized she didn't look well. She had the haggard face of a person that hadn't slept for days. He wondered if it was something worse than that. Had Hunter done something horrible to her?

Jules didn't speak, but instead threw a photograph down onto the bed between David's legs. "Why didn't you tell me you had a wife? All this time I believed you loved me." She was crying.

He looked up at her with sympathetic eyes. "Jules, I'm so sorry. I didn't want to hurt you. Come on, Jules, help me out of here. We're running out of time."

Jules reached around her back and pulled out a gun from where it had been hidden in her waistband. Her face was expressionless.

"Jules, no. Don't shoot me!" David cried. "My wife's probably long dead. Almost everyone is. What was the point in telling you about her, when she's already dead?"

She leveled the gun and aimed it at David's chest, the gun shaking in her hand. Then she turned it around and slid the muzzle into her mouth, and with tears rolling down her face, she squeezed the trigger. As the gunshot echoed off the walls, Prof. Hunter rushed in.

"No! Look what you've done?" Prof. Hunter shook his head. "The poor girl. It's too bad she shot herself in the head. She must have wasted enough brain matter to control half a dozen walkers. Oh well, live and let live, right? Or in this case…die." He chuckled, a wicked grin creasing his face. "Now, will you do as I wish, David? There's no reason not to now."

David could only sob as he nodded his head in capitulation. He'd always wanted to be a leader, in command of many men.

He just thought they would have been alive.

THE EVE OF ZOMPIRES

CANDIS VARGO

I walked through the deserted streets looking for any sign of recent life. My fist clenched a silver cross that doubled as a dagger. I refused to let my guard down. I've made that mistake before, which was one time too many. I gently walked through the rubble from the ruined buildings that filled the streets. The smell of human decay and ashes from the fires that had gone out long ago filled every breath I took. It's all that was left of New Orleans.

There were no signs of recent activity in this town. Whatever survivors there were, they took everything they could long ago. When word spread, so did the riots. I'll never understand why people will steal luxury items and run around like maniacs when they know they're going to die anyway. The moment people realized the world was changing, all humanity was thrown out.

With two hours until sunset, I needed to find a safe haven for the night. I began looking around for a police station or a hospital with at least one section of solid walls. When I came across an old insane asylum, it wasn't exactly what I had in mind, but it would work. All I needed was one solid room with a strong door to secure my safety for the night and enough windows in the outer rooms to keep the demons away when the sun rose.

I made my way into the old asylum. As I passed an old, cracked mirror, I saw my reflection and I barely recognized myself. My once shaved face was covered in a thick beard and my hair was in desperate need of cutting. My brown skin was covered in dirt. Soon, I came across a padded room with a solid metal door. I figured if it can hold crazy people, then it should be able to keep the demons out. I was going to attempt to find something to place in front of the door to hold it closed, maybe some chains strapped around it or a large heavy desk in front of it, when I noticed several locks bolted on the inside of the door. It was a sign of someone staying here, but I assumed they had left long ago, either by leaving the city or becoming one of *them*. After locking myself in the room, I pocketed my dagger and removed my backpack. I took out my last box of granola bars and tore it apart so I could use it to cover the small window about head-height on the door. As long as those things couldn't hear or see me, I would be safe.

I sat down in a corner in the back of the small, rectangular room and breathed out a sigh of relief. There was refuse scattered about he floor; another sign that someone had been staying here.

I never imagined this would actually happen. I wouldn't say it was an apocalypse, but it was certainly the end as humanity knew it. You were either a meal or you became one of the beasts if they thought they could use you. More reasons for me to stay away. I'd rather die than become one of the living dead.

I was jolted from my thoughts when I heard the thud of footsteps echoing in the asylum outside my safe room. My heart quickened and muscles tensed. The footsteps started out slow, but it only took a moment for them to move at full speed.

No. It's not even sunset yet. How is this possible? I thought.

When the footsteps stopped outside my room, a steady pounding began on the door. I took a step forward and leaned my head closer. The pounding came again, followed by raspy breathing. I jerked my head back and my heart quickened in my chest. This shouldn't be possible. It wasn't supposed to be like this. There was an hour left until the sun went down and there were more than enough windows out in the hallway to let the light in. How would one, just one, have managed to find me and begin banging on the door?

The thuds on the door came again, more fierce this time. In one bold move, I reached up and tore the cardboard away from the small window. The last thing I expected to see was the face of a woman, who was severely pissed off, with a double-barreled shotgun pointed at the window.

"Who the hell are you?" the woman demanded.

"Does it really matter who I am? You're the first person I've seen in a long time that isn't one of *them*. Where did you come from?" I asked.

"Will you at least open the damn door?"

"If you lower the gun." What did she think I was, stupid?

After a long pause, she lowered the shotgun and said, "Better?"

Before I unlocked the door, I reached down and clasped my dagger, still refusing to let my guard down. I stood behind the door as I opened it, prepared for her to whip the gun up and point it at me. I didn't know if I was more surprised or curious when she didn't.

I didn't realize I was staring at her until she said, "Are you gonna close that door or not? Quite frankly, I'd prefer if you did. There's only twenty minutes until they come out and I want to stay alive."

"Twenty minutes? It's almost an hour until sunset," I said.

"Yeah well, you obviously didn't get a good look behind the building. With the larger ones back there it gets dark here faster. Like I said: twenty minutes."

"So who are you?" I asked after I locked the door and placed the cardboard back on the window.

"Name's Sarah. You?"

"Jerome. Where did you come from? I've been walking through this town all day and haven't seen a damn soul."

"I'm just that good at hiding. I've been staying in this room since the virus, or whatever it is."

Trust is a hard thing to give in this world now, but I wanted to know how much she knew about what lurked in the darkness. Looking at her, I could tell she'd been alone for a while. Her clothes were torn and dirty. They were so worn you could hardly see her slim figure underneath. Even though her dark hair was tied up in a ponytail, I could tell it was greasy from her not having showered in a long time. Sarah watched me warily with her hazel eyes as I went to a corner and sat down.

"A virus? That's what you think it is?"

"That's what they started to tell everyone," she said and sat down in the opposite corner. "When I realized they only came out at night, I thought they were vampires. That is, until I heard wooden stakes and garlic wouldn't do the trick. Honestly, I have no clue what they are."

"That's all you've got? A virus or *vampires*? Really?"

"Oh, I'm so sorry, Jerome, that I'm not an expert on things that try to kill me at night."

No one must have come through this town for a while. If she still didn't know what they were, she must not have seen another person in months. Everyone I'd met since the plague had the right idea; they just didn't know the complete facts.

"Vampires aren't real," I stated. "At least not the ones you're thinking of."

"Could have fooled me. Something that wants to eat you and only comes out at night; kind of sounds like one to me."

"They're more like zombies."

Sarah looked at me as if I truly belonged in this place. As if I was crazy. How naïve she was. Everyone always assumes when it comes to reality, Hollywood had it right. That's why the majority of humans either became infected or dinner when it all began.

When the word spread, everyone thought they were safe in their homes. As long as they stayed quiet, they thought they would survive.

"Yeah, and I'm Santa Claus," she laughed.

"You could believe they were vampires, but not zombies? How so?"

"Zombies are slow and they want to eat your brains. They don't only come out at night."

"You know, I'm surprised you've stayed alive this long," I said. "We're not talking about movie zombies. We're talking about real ones. The ones that are about to try and get to us in the next ten minutes. Have you even tried to kill one of them?"

"Maybe if I knew how, I would. I didn't even know they were zombies until you just said it. If that's true, then they're pretty damn fast for zombies. But all I have to do is slice off their heads or shoot out their brains, right?"

Sarah was in for a rude awakening and I told her as much. "Zombies are harder to kill than you think. It's not like in the movies where you can get close enough to slice their heads off with a meat cleaver and you sure as hell don't get a magical box with weapons. This isn't a video game. If you get that close to one they drag their nails across your skin, tearing through the flesh and muscle, in one single swipe. You could attempt to shoot them from a distance, but I wouldn't recommend it. If you do that you expose yourself to others who will hear the gunshot. As fun as the movie zombies were, they had it all wrong. They're a type of demon. Imagine a vampire and a zombie with demon abilities. Hollywood couldn't have gotten it more wrong. Both a vampire and a zombie bite you, they want your blood and flesh, and they can infect you and turn you into one of them. Neither one have an expiration date and they're both the living dead. They're kind of one in the same, but they are demons. Think about it. Anything that rises from the dead is caused by one of two things; either by witchcraft or the devil. The only good thing that ever came back was Jesus, and that sure as hell isn't him out there."

"You're fucking with me, right?" Sarah asked.

"Sorry, no I'm not. Now if they're about to come out, we need to shut our damn mouths and be ready. You said you've been here for how long?"

"Almost six months."

"So this door should hold. We need to rest if we can. I'll be on the move again in the morning and I need to get *some* sleep. Those things can hear us as soon as they wake. When the sun comes up we can talk then. By the way, I call them *zompires*," I said with a smirk.

Sarah's face, if at all possible, was even paler than it was when I first saw her. I watched as she wrapped her arms around her knees like a child would do if they were watching a horror movie. Within the terror of her face, I saw confusion as she tried to grasp the information I'd just told her, and not knowing if she could trust me or the concept of reality. I didn't plan on scaring her but she needed to know the facts. There wasn't any easy way for her to kill them.

A part of me felt bad for her. Sarah had been alone, fighting an unknown force for six months. She's been fighting a losing battle. There wasn't a single human who could take those things down. I knew I was her only hope. I wanted to take her under my wing and protect her but that would only slow me down. I didn't know how she managed to survive this long, as most of the humans had already disappeared. Maybe I could just take her with me until I came across another group of people.

The more I thought about it, the more I realized she was better off with me.

I didn't know if she could be trusted. I didn't know anything about her, but something told me I needed to keep her with me. If there's one thing I've learned about my kind, it's to always trust my instinct.

I pulled my revolver out of my bag and put it next to me—better safe than sorry. I hoped I could get some sleep tonight as I rested my head on my bag. I held my dagger in one hand and my revolver in the other, prepared for anything that should happen. When I could hear the sound of hundreds of footsteps rumbling out in the street, I clasped my weapons tighter and closed my eyes.

When I awoke, I listened for any signs of them on the street but everything was as quiet as a cold winter day in the forest. I looked over at Sarah and she was still curled, sleeping. Quietly sitting up, I reached in my backpack and took out two bottles of water. I leaned forward and tapped Sarah on the arm with one.

"Hey, wake up."

With one swift and clumsy motion, she sat up. She began moving her head around like she'd forgotten where she was. "They're gone?"

"It's morning. I don't hear anything, so my guess is yes."

"Water? Where'd you get it?" she asked and grabbed the bottle. She opened it and began to take large gulps.

"Slow down. It has to last. People forget to look in basements of houses when they're raiding. Let's get out of here so we can wash up."

"There's no place to wash. I've checked everywhere in this town and there isn't running water anywhere. No generators either."

I cocked her half a smile. "Come on."

I pulled away a side of the cardboard and looked out the window on the door. There was light shining all around, so I put the cardboard back in my bag and we headed out.

"Where's the closest restaurant?" I asked.

"Two blocks down. Why? There's no food there. I just told you I've been all around this town. Two days ago I took the last of what was in a vending machine back on Saints Street."

I ignored her as I walked in the direction of the restaurant. For some reason, people only think of water as a way of getting clean.

We walked into an old family diner that had all the windows smashed. No doubt from the riots. When people realized humanity was going to be extinct, they took it upon themselves to trash whatever they could. Maybe they thought it would be something fun for them to do before they died or they could have been just a bunch of idiots. Stealing anything they could just so they could die owning a large television or an expensive car seemed foolish to me. It wasn't until the world was almost gone that they decided to start stealing food.

I looked through all of the ruins in the restaurant. I searched underneath every table that was turned over and all of the shards of glass from the dishes. When I went to the back, I found what I needed on the floor in a pantry.

"Here." I handed Sarah some moist towelettes.

"Seriously?"

"You don't need water to get cleaned up. Hold onto them and we'll go find you a change of clothes."

"I've already…"

"I know. You've already looked everywhere and there isn't any. You looked for the obvious in the obvious spots. Just like everyone else. You need to look in the not so obvious places."

"So what are we looking for now, Mr. Know It All?"

"I saw a hotel up ahead. We'll go there."

When we walked into the hotel lobby, Sarah was more than confused when I led her into the basement and through several doors. When we finally made it to the laundry room, we dug through clothes until we found something that would decently fit us. The hotel had a laundry service for guests. We hung up a sheet to separate us so we could clean ourselves off with the towelettes as best we could and get changed.

"You done?" I asked after I'd changed into a pair of jeans and a white t-shirt.

"Yeah." She walked around the hanging sheet. She was dressed in clothes that fit better. With a pair of nice sweat pants and blue shirt, she looked pretty.

"So, where are you headed?" she asked.

"Just over the bridge to Eden Isle. I'm sure that bridge is blown to shit so we'll have to find a boat and try to make it across."

"Why are you taking me with you?"

"Honestly, I don't know. You've been alone for a while and maybe you just need some help."

"Okay. Well, what's on Eden Isle?"

"Our only true safe haven. You wouldn't understand."

"Try me."

"I'm sure you've heard of the Garden of Eden."

I knew she wouldn't understand. She began laughing uncontrollably as she held her stomach. "You expect me to believe that's the Garden of Eden?" She attempted to catch her breath from laughing so hard.

"I don't expect you to believe shit. I'm just telling you what I know. That's where we're going and we have until the eclipse happens to get there."

That sure as hell got her attention. The blood drained from her face as she slowly said, "What eclipse?"

"You really don't know much about the end of times, do you?"

"No, not really. Now what damn eclipse?" she demanded.

I was kind of glad I'd struck a nerve with her. Now maybe she'd take me more seriously.

"Well, when the sun goes down tonight, it won't be coming back up in the morning. It's the permanent eclipse. It's when evil will roam freely. They'll attempt to get into Eden by using their human minions and only the chosen can protect it. That's why I need to go. That'll be the only place where the sun doesn't stop shining until eventually the demons die from not being able to feed off of blood. That could take several hundreds of years, but we'll be able to live there for our lives anyway. The Garden of Eden has everything we'll need."

After a long moment of silence for Sarah to gather her thoughts, she said, "Okay, I'm not saying I believe you completely. But if there's the slightest possibility of surviving this shit… then let's go."

I began to empty my bag of everything except my weapons, water, and ammunition. I left a few granola bars in there after we each ate one. I knew we were going to have to get some ground underneath our feet and we'd need all of the energy we could get. I studied Sarah as she loaded her shotgun and I started to wonder how she'd survived this long. I knew how I had, but her I didn't understand. How could a helpless human survive for so long with the creatures we were fighting?

Finding a boat took longer than expected. Of course, all of the motor boats and row boats were gone or floating in the middle of the lake. We finally found a paddle boat that looked about thirty years old. It was either take the paddle boat or go around the lake on foot. It would take more than a day to go on foot and we didn't have the time to spare.

"Hop in." I gestured for Sarah to get in the boat after I'd gotten it in the water.

"Christ. Can't anything be easy for us?" she said as she climbed in.

I laughed. "Unfortunately not. We have to deal with what we have."

"Will we make it in time?"

"If you move your feet fast enough." We began paddling.

"So what's your story?" she asked as she paddled. "And where are you from? Mexico or something?"

"Just because my skin is dark doesn't mean I'm from Mexico. I'm Puerto Rican but I've lived in America since I was three. My mom and dad died when I was seventeen. I have no siblings. What about you?"

"In and out of foster homes since I was a kid. Everyone kept saying I did things that I didn't. Finally, when I was sixteen, I ran away. No one ever bothered looking for me."

"What kind of things did they say you did?" Now this was starting to peak my interest. Maybe somehow this will tell me why I felt drawn to her. Why I felt like I needed to protect her.

"Well, when I was seven, the family I was staying with said I made a flower grow out of the tiles in the bathroom. I swear they were all crazy. Every family said something wild and unbelievable, yet the state made me switch homes anyway. Nothing like feeling unwanted. They used to say my birthmark would glow at night. Maybe they were all doped up or something."

The mention of her birthmark glowing sent chills down my spine. I knew I was drawn to protect her, but she couldn't be the one. It was nearly impossible.

"Can I see?"

She looked at me, confused.

"Your birthmark," I said.

"Yeah, sure." Sarah turned her back toward me and pulled her shirt down over one shoulder. I looked at the birthmark. It resembled a snake slithering across her shoulder. When I reached out to touch it, I felt a shock jolt through my body and all of my muscles tensed. Images of a tree and a snake flashed before my eyes and I knew exactly what it meant. She *was* the one.

I knew understanding all of this would ensure my reasoning to protect her, but I didn't understand why she'd been sent to me. With the burning desire to wrap her in my embrace and keep her away from all of the creatures roaming the Earth, I felt like I now would be more of a temptation for her. Or maybe that's just what she was to me. When the complete existence of mankind depended on her, I couldn't let myself fall for such temptation. I couldn't allow myself be drawn to her as anything more than the one I needed to protect.

Feeling my pulse quicken and my body heat rise, I turned around and continued to paddle the boat. I didn't understand why I felt like this. I didn't necessarily want to indulge in sex with her, but instead I simply wanted to hold her and gently kiss her lips. I thought about it. I thought about what it would feel like to have her in my arms. I was both grateful and disappointed when the sound of her voice cut off my thoughts.

"What's that smell?"

"Death."

Sarah gasped when she looked around in the water. There were chunks of human flesh and hollow bones floating in the red-tinted lake. Apparently, the zompires didn't just want to eat flesh and drink your blood. They also wanted to suck the marrow out of human bones.

"We're almost there," I said.

"Good because if we have to go through this much longer I think I'm going to hurl."

As we got closer to the shore, we paddled through the human remains floating around our boat. We got as close as we could before the boat hit the shore and I wasn't going to make her walk through the remains. I carried her to the shore and put her down once I was out of any meat chunks of flesh that had washed up onto the shore.

"How much farther is it?" she asked.

"Just a couple of miles. There's still five hours until the sun goes down. We should be able to make it."

Unease passed over me as I looked around. Something about this place was unsettling. Whatever it was, it wasn't good.

"What are you…"

"Shhh."

I needed her to be quiet so I could listen to the sounds in the distance. There was something out there that was watching us and going to attack, I could feel it. I readied my revolver and grasped my dagger.

"Your shotgun is loaded, right?" I asked in a whisper, so whoever was out there wouldn't hear.

"Yeah, why? Jerome, what's going on?"

"Don't use it unless you have to but be ready. We're being watched, and whoever it is isn't alone. Stay beside me and when they come, don't try to be a hero. Leave that to me."

The look of fear passed over her face as her grip tightened on the shotgun. She gave me a quick nod. I could tell she hadn't had to face any of their minions before. They're the humans who were promised not to be harmed as long as they captured people and took them to the demons. I don't know how anyone could believe such crap. What did they think would happen once there wasn't anyone left except for them?

We didn't walk for five minutes before they sprang for an attack. There were three of them together, with switchblades in their hands. They were filthy and had a crazed look on their faces. You could tell they haven't had anything to eat for a long time because there wasn't much to them.

I instantly took a protective stance in front of Sarah as they stood in a line in front of us. With their knives pointed out in front of them, they glared at us, laughing. It was the laugh only a crazed maniac could use.

"We're kind of in a hurry, fellas. So if you don't mind, we'd like to keep going," I said.

"You're going somewhere all right. You're going with us," the guy in the middle cackled. I figured he must be the leader of the group. He was the tallest and the one with the most meat on his bones. Since he'd spoken first, I knew the others weren't nearly as important.

"Whatever it is you want, I assure you…we don't have it." I thought if I played stupid, it would increase my chances when the fighting began. Maybe they wouldn't realize I knew exactly what they wanted and what they were going to try to do.

"Give us your weapons and come with us. You have to be alive when we bring you in," another one said.

"We're not going anywhere," I said a matter-of-factly.

As soon as those words left my lips, two of the minions came forward to attack. I grabbed the first one by the wrist and twisted it until I heard it snap. At the same time I kicked the second one in the chest, knocking the air out of him. The second one stumbled backwards and fell to the ground. I used my dagger to stab the first one in the jugular before I let him fall, lifeless, to the pavement. I tried not to notice Sarah as she stared at the soulless body bleeding out on the ground. She must have never seen a human kill another before. But then again, I wasn't quite human.

I glanced at the second one, who was still lying on the ground, and I assumed he was unconscious, so I advanced on the leader. When I was close enough to him, he pulled a pistol out from behind his back and pointed it at my forehead. Lucky for me, I was bigger and faster. I knocked the gun out of his hand in one swift move as I wrapped his arm around his head and twisted myself to where I was standing behind him. I was about to snap his neck when I heard a faint whisper, "Jerome."

The moment I recognized Sarah's voice, I released the leader and spun around, ready to attack. There she was, the woman I vowed to protect, in the arms of the man I thought was unconscious. He had the barrel of her shotgun pressed into her temple. I hid my dagger underneath my clothing before he saw it in my hand. No way was he going to take it from me.

"That's right, pretty boy. Now I can tell you don't want her to die, so you're best bet is to come with me. Drop your gun, now."

I hesitated.

"Do it or she's dead."

I threw my revolver on the ground.

"I'm sorry. I just…I didn't see him," Sarah said.

"It's okay. I'll take care of this," I reassured her.

The leader punched me in the gut for good measure, and as I sucked in air from the blow to my stomach, the two minions led me and Sarah away, leaving their brother dead on the ground.

I didn't know if she knew where they were going to take us. Hell, I wasn't exactly sure where. I knew they were going to take us to the beasts we were trying to outrun.

The last place I expected to go was an old factory. As soon as we walked inside, I could hear Sarah's breath begin to shake at the horror before us. The zompires weren't just killing off the humans. They were herding them like cattle.

The smell of death was overpowering and the heat was fierce. It felt like I had just walked into a solid wall of souls trying to escape. There were several humans lined up with a chain bound around their feet.

That started the line.

As the line moved forward, the chains would yank the humans straight up so they were hanging upside down. There were rows of minions who would then break the necks of the humans, and drain their blood into barrels for the demons to feast on like the blood was fine wine. From there it was too grotesque for even me to look. They hacked away at the bodies, separating the meat from the bones.

If it were under any better circumstances, I would have commented on Sarah's ability to hold back from vomiting, because I sure wanted to throw up. I glanced over at her. She focused her gaze on the floor, not daring to look up. I didn't blame her.

We were taken into a room on the top of the building. Every window was covered in metal, to be sure not to let any light in. In the back of the room, I saw him. Sitting in a chair covered in red velvet, was the leader of these minions. The minions left Sarah and me alone with him, locking the door when they left.

With blood staining his mouth and chin, the leader looked up and smiled. Every one of his teeth was pointed and reminded me of a shark. His eyes were blackened with a blood red ring surrounding them. His skin was as white as an albino's, with tears across them that were rotting from the inside. He lifted up a long, skinny finger and pointed a razor sharp fingernail at me and Sarah.

"Ah. I see you've brought me something extraordinary." The words slithered out of his mouth. "A Nephilim and you," he said while looking at Sarah. "You were their only hope. Too bad."

He reached over and grabbed a femur from a glass dish next to his seat and began to suck the marrow out of it. The sound of his slurping made Sarah gag in disgust.

"What do you mean I was their only hope?" Sarah asked after she forced the vomit back down her throat.

"Oh, your little Nephilim didn't tell you? You my dear…are their Eve."

"Yeah," she laughed. "And you must be Frankenstein."

I had to admit, for someone who didn't know much about things, she sure had some balls.

"It's true," I said. "When I saw your birthmark, I knew it was true. You're the Eve of our time and the only hope to rebuilding the human race after the demons die off. And I'm a Nephilim, just like he said. A half Angel born to protect Eden."

"Well, if that's true, then you're doing a shitty ass job of it," Sarah said angrily.

She had every right to say that. To think it. I'd thought all hope was lost once we were locked in here with the zompire, too. My back began to itch, and knowing what it meant, I knew there was only one way out of here, and we were going to take it.

"Yes, a Nephilim who is still a newborn. You haven't come in to your abilities yet and you are still weak. Such a waist for your kind, but wonderful for me," the demon said. Every word he uttered made my stomach crawl with hate.

The moment he leaped to attack, he screeched hideously. His cheeks split in half as he readied himself to kill Sarah. My shoulder blades shook with pain as my skin tore apart, allowing for my wings to break through. Once my wings were exposed, I spun around and knocked him away from Sarah. I wrapped Sarah in my wings behind my back as I advanced on the zompire.

"Yeah, too bad they decided to finally give me my wings. Now you're shit out of luck."

He let out another screech and lunged for me, attempting to bite out my throat. I pulled my dagger from where I'd hidden it and sliced the blade across his throat. Blood as black as his soul flowed down his chest, and he grabbed his throat and collapsed.

"Yeah, that's right. The Holy Dagger. Very useful against bastards like you." I released Sarah from my wings as I leaned down and stuck the dagger into the zompire's heart. I watched as he began to convulse and the smell of decay radiated from his body.

I wasn't aware of Sarah screaming until I pulled the dagger out of the zompire's chest.

"Sarah! It's okay." I firmly grasped her shoulders as I tried to look her in the eyes. "We need to go. Calm down and hold on to me."

She stopped screaming once I tore the metal off the window to let the little bit of sunlight in. I knew it wouldn't be long until the minions tried to come after us, so I swept Sarah up in my arms and jumped out of the window.

At first I thought we were in trouble as my wings were new, but a second later instinct took over and we were flying through the air.

Sarah finally calmed down enough to yell at me. "You have wings and we've been walking this whole damn time! You could have flown us over that lake with no problem! What the hell?"

"I just received them. Could you imagine a bunch of young Nephilim with wings? They'd be flying around all over the place and expose us all."

She grunted in reply and tightened her arms around my neck. "So, I'm the great Eve, huh? What does that mean? I get to mate with a lot of men to create babies?"

I laughed and said, "No, that's not how you're going to rebuild the human race. You're going to create all on the Earth which the zompires have destroyed. I'm sure those in Eden will have no problem taking care of that. You'll rebuild nature. You hold the elements of the Earth. Earth, wind, fire and water. You'll bring it all back to life."

"Oh, well, that's a lot better than what I was thinking."

Once we landed in the safety of the Garden of Eden, I gave into my yearning I'd held in for so long. Before I set her down, I leaned in and kissed her soft, delicate lips.

I was both shocked and relieved when she kissed me back.

This is it, I thought. *This is where I belong. She is my Eve, and I am her Adam.*

There was still along way to go, but soon, the demons and zompires would perish, and then, life would begin again.

THE ROOM WHERE SHE SLEEPS

JENNIFER KOEHLER

Just before daylight she awoke in the room where she slept. The suffocating pre-dawn darkness befriended the deafening silence that hung in the air. The weight of both was soul crushing. She'd spent hours listening to the silence in her room and the world beyond its walls. Months had passed since any human sounds, other than her own, had drifted past her ear. Sounds she'd once found annoying she would now give anything to hear again: a blaring car horn, an out of tune whistle, the stentorian roar of baseball fans in a crowded stadium. She would have given even more to hear the clinking of glass and forks in a busy restaurant, the vibration of a cell phone, or the innocent laughter of a child.

Months had passed and cars have stopped racing up and down the neighborhood streets, their drivers in a hurry to live life. No one was left to whistle an out of tune song, blare a horn or yell scathing taunts at a batter. The once joyful screams of the neighborhood kids running along the sidewalk while playing hide and seek had turned into screams of terror and pain—then the screams had stopped and the moaning began.

Even the birds and crickets had grown silent.

Every once in a while, if she listened closely and the ringing in her ears stopped, she could hear the dead shuffling past her bedroom window. They moaned softly to themselves, as if trying to comfort their insatiable supernatural hunger.

She pondered the room where she slept as it filled with pre-dawn light, and sighed.

The house was quiet with emptiness.

As the sun rose in the sky, a single ray of sunshine illuminated the bedroom, causing the roses painted on the white plaster walls to glow with a crimson luminosity. Large and voluptuous, the full blooms appeared to sway in the breeze with drops of dew clinging to their petals' tips—desperate to retain their teardrop figures. Green thorny branches, interwoven in a razor-sharp lattice, barely kept the heavy blooms from submitting to gravity. A few accepting defeat have fallen to the plush grass beneath their lofty perches among the thorns, their petals strewn about as if carelessly plucked for a 'he loves me, he loves me not' scenario.

Ryan had painted the roses—her favorite flower—one rainy weekend while she was away. He'd painted them with great care and meticulous detail. They looked so much like the real thing that she often felt like the bedroom was her own personal rose garden.

"I'll never have to buy you roses again," he'd laughed.

She sighed.

Ryan was gone.

Two weeks ago, he'd left to find sparkplugs for the generator. His paranoid mind had prepared for everything: food, water, batteries, even tampons to last the rest of her life—but not plugs for a broken generator. The nearest automotive store was fifteen miles away. At the most he should have been gone a day. Two weeks meant…

She was growing tired of the anxious knot in her stomach. Never has he been gone this long. Never in their five years together have they been apart for more than two days.

"Stay," she'd pleaded, as they stood at the kitchen door that opened to the backyard. He'd only kissed her softly on the lips and embraced her. She'd rested her head on his shoulder and kissed him on the neck just below his chiseled jawline, his day-old stubble tickling her lips. "Please don't go," she'd whispered. "We can survive without the generator. I can't survive without you." He'd kissed her one last time before walking out the door, through the backyard gate.

Again she sighed.

A succinct rumbled meow with a dash of purr, pulls her away from the roses. Mr. Kitty, her white cat with emerald eyes was sitting at the foot of the bed in a patch of yellow sunlight. He knew the exact time and place to catch some rays from the one window in the room. He was a sun whore. His white fur blinded her tired eyes as he meowed again.

"I gotcha, kit cat, you're hungry," she said and dragged herself out of bed.

In a flash, Mr. Kitty ran to the kitchen as she slowly followed behind.

She fed her beloved cat and returned to the bedroom. She opened the large trunk on the floor at the foot of the bed. The trunk was filled with various weapons and enough ammunition to wipe out a small city—she picked the AR-15 rifle and two spare, fully-loaded magazines. Each room of the house held a similar trunk, but the real stash was hidden in a subterranean storage room Ryan had built beneath the basement floor.

With the stealth and grace of a cheetah stalking its prey, she quietly tied back the curtain and raised the Venetian blinds. She opened the window with an enduring squeak that echoed through the empty neighborhood. One by one their heads slowly turned in her direction.

She loaded one of the thirty-round magazines into her favorite gun and positioned herself at the bedroom window. On their first date, Ryan had taken her to a private shooting range owned by a mutual friend who'd lived far past the city limits. When he'd pulled an AR-15 out of the trunk of his 1967 Chevy Impala, she'd known Ryan was the one and only man for her. Two months after that first date she had her own AR-15 because, he'd said, "A beautiful woman deserved a beautiful gun."

The afternoon sun filled the room with a golden glow as she peered through the scope. A warm summer breeze carried a rancid stench through the window. Mr. Kitty, distracted from grooming his paws, raised his aristocratic nose and sniffed the air. He sneezed as he nonchalantly pranced out of the room. The breeze agitated the leaves on the large oak tree in the northwest corner of her backyard. The leaves whispered to the wind in anticipation.

The second story window provided the perfect vantage point for taking out the undead. She flipped the safety with her right thumb.

She counted twenty zombies roaming the large backyard, aimless and insatiably hungry. A few unable to navigate the four-foot stone and brick wall that bordered the property stood blocked. Unable to move forward, they simply stopped, too dumb to turn around and walk in the other direction. At the back of the yard, two zombies stood, trampling her rose bushes, on either side of the wall, facing each other and unaware of the other's existence. The wrought iron gate next to the pair was open. The broken latch—a long forgotten chore that seemed all too important now.

She sighed.

A few zombies shuffled along the yard, while others stood in place and stared at nothing. She wondered what a zombie saw, if anything. Their dead milky white eyes, devoid of anything human, sent shivers down her spine. Their bodies were bruised, ripped open with entrails dragging on the ground below. Some were naked, missing chunks of flesh down to the bone, their skin tattooed with purplish black spider veins, thick black pus oozing from their wounds.

Slowly, she panned the scope across the backyard, looking for her first kill. She recognized some of her neighbors, but others she didn't know at all.

She settled her sights on Mr. Jensen, her retired next-door neighbor. He was a meticulous old man in his sixties with a white handlebar mustache and tinted transition glasses. He enjoyed yelling at the neighborhood kids as they ran through his yard with reckless abandon. "Stupid little hoodlums," he'd called them. But for her it was, "Pretty young thing."

His trademark jeans and white polo shirt were covered in dirt, dried blood, and black pus. His shirt was torn at the right shoulder where he was missing a large portion of skin and muscle. The wound wept with black pus, and like a slow river, filled with sludge and ran down his arm and to his fingertips.

Drip.

Drip.

Drip—onto the green grass at his feet.

His sluggish arms rose as he took a step toward the house. She squeezed the trigger. Once. Twice. Mr. Jensen's head exploded and his body dropped to the ground. The gunshots echoed throughout the vacant neighborhood. The heads of the remaining zombies snapped out of their stupor and focused their milky dead eyes on the house. Their arms stretched out before them as they started to moan—softly at first. With each step their moans grew louder.

Methodically she took each one out. After her third kill, more zombies appeared at the edges of her once beautifully landscaped backyard. Two more dead zombies and she was in her happy place—zoning out as she robotically executed one zombie after the other. On automatic pilot she watched as once human faces surrendered to the force of the .223 Remington bullets. Brains exploded from their heads and bone was shattered as she thought of her first date with Ryan. She paused only to reload.

The memory replayed in her mind as if it was happening for the first time. She was sitting at a makeshift, but sturdy, wooden table—the AR-15 was resting in front of her, patiently waiting to reveal its awesome power. Ryan stood close behind, the scent of his cologne and the heat of his body swirling in the air between them. His touch was intoxicating as he ran his hands along her bare arms, guiding her into the correct posture. She refrained from telling him this wasn't her first time with an AR-15 and allowed him to instruct her. She took her time setting her sights and getting her bearings. The warm summer afternoon air was calm and quiet. The only sound was her blood rushing through her ears as the adrenaline built up. Her breath quickened and finally, the target was in sight with Ryan waiting in anticipation to her right; she squeezed the trigger. The gunfire reverberated in her core as every cell in her body vibrated with each exploding bullet. The gunfire echoed in the distance as it bounced off the surrounding hills. She emptied the magazine, looked at Ryan, and gave him her most brilliant smile. A look of wonder mixed with desire filled his radiant blue eyes as he took her into his arms. Their first kiss, tasting of bittersweet copper and gunpowder, was deeply passionate and she knew the rest of her life would be spent with him. Wherever his soul traveled, hers would always be with his—dead or alive.

Her happy place dissolved into the past, and reality came into focus, and forty zombies lay dead under the warm afternoon sun.

She scanned the yard with her scope, looking for her next mark. A man with shaggy blonde hair, six feet tall, wearing biker boots, jeans, and plain white t-shirt was standing in the open gate. She'd recognize his thin muscular frame anywhere. She dropped the gun on the bed and ran from the room. She raced through the house and out the back door, then rushed into the yard. Ryan was home.

She ran to him anxious to be engulfed by his strong arms—to rest an ear against his chest and be mesmerized by his heartbeat—to feel whole again.

She slipped and fell into a gelatinous puddle of brains and black pus as Ryan remained standing at the open gate. She picked herself up and continued on. She was ten feet from Ryan when she saw his eyes—milky white.

Dead. Lifeless.

The fight in her soul jumped off the proverbial cliff as she fell to the ground before him. Her heart skipped a few beats as her lungs deflated—the air sucked out by an unseen and sinister force. She gasped for air, but like a stubborn child, her lungs refused to cooperate.

Ryan moaned and took a step in her direction. Denial retains its grasp on her, as she remained motionless. Another step—his moan turned deep, guttural. Desperate.

Her breath returned as she breathed in the rancid stink of the black pus on her skin. His dead milky eyes stared blankly into hers. Still she couldn't move.

One more step and she wouldn't have to live through this horror any longer. Ryan stood above her, his arms outstretched. He reached for her. His putrid flesh grazed her cheek just as a white streak of fur slammed into his chest.

It took a split second for her to realize the big ball of puffed-out white fur attacking Ryan was Mr. Kitty.

"Mr. Kitty! No!"

The cat growled and spit in Ryan's face, his claws ripped away chunks of flesh as he climbed Ryan like a tree. Ryan sluggishly reached for the cat, but he was too slow.

Her wits about her again, she rose to her feet as Mr. Kitty sank his claws into Ryan's once beautiful face. She grabbed the cat by the scruff of the neck, pulled him to her chest, and ran as fast as she could back to the house. Mr. Kitty growled and hissed over her shoulder as Ryan's moans grew louder. She heard his footsteps shuffle through the grass. After a shuffle or two, it turned into full-on running.

"Holy shit, Mr. Kitty! They can run!"

The cat growled in response as she picked up speed. A hundred feet more and she'd be safe. Ryan's steps were getting closer, his moans louder. Fifty feet and she could feel his fingertips touch her hair. Mr. Kitty lashed out with a paw.

Thirty feet and her lungs were burning—her mind wild with adrenaline. Her heart felt ready to burst through her ribcage as Ryan took hold of her t-shirt.

She screamed and clutched her beloved cat to her chest. Twenty feet—she strained against his pull as the fabric tore.

She felt it give and stumbled forward.

Ten feet, five and she was throwing Mr. Kitty into the kitchen and slamming the door in her dead boyfriend's face. She turned the lock—force of habit—and quickly replaced the wooden barricade across the door. The steel door wasn't thick enough to keep out Ryan's ravenous moans.

Mr. Kitty let out a long, bellowing meow—his eyes were wild, his fur standing on end.

"Mr. Kitty, the blowfish cat," she said. "Come here, kit cat."

The cat huffed like a bull as she approached. He crawled into her lap and started to purr. She burst into tears and gathered the cat to her chest. The cat turned into a rag doll and allowed her to grieve. He placed a paw on her hand and meowed a soft, rumbled meow. For what seemed like an eternity she cried. Mr. Kitty purred, and for the moment it was all they needed.

Finally, as the sun set and the house grew dark, her tears subsided. Ryan moaned outside the kitchen door and Mr. Kitty was ready to be set free. She grabbed a flashlight from a kitchen drawer and together they retreated into the basement. She grabbed a ten-gallon jug of water and carried it to the master bath on the second floor. When the first signs of zombies began popping up, Ryan had been prepared, as was she—because she loved him she'd entertained his paranoia. She'd never believed in the apocalypse let alone a *zombie* apocalypse.

She believed in Ryan and that was enough for her. But now…

He'd rigged a camping shower to the existing shower and stored enough water to last a lifetime. She attached the water jug to the portable water heater and let it warm as she undressed. She threw her ruined clothes into the trashcan.

"We'll burn those later. Won't we, kit cat?"

The cat only looked at her in response. She picked him up and carried him into the shower with her. He hissed in protest.

She turned on the water and removed bits of Ryan's zombie flesh from the cat's claws. She soaped him up and washed the sticky black pus from his white fur. Once clean, she released him—much to his satisfaction—and he ran dripping out of the bathroom to nurse his bruised ego.

She furiously scrubbed her skin until it was red. She cleaned every crease and fold of her body. She washed her hair multiple times before she felt clean of the rancid zombie stink.

Clean and smelling of rose-scented soap, she retired to the room where she slept.

She unloaded the AR-15 and returned it to the trunk. Before closing the lid, she pulled out Ryan's standard police issue 9mm Glock. Never in his ten years as an officer did he fire the gun.

She sat on the trunk and turned off the flashlight. The darkness took hold with its suffocating grasp as Ryan's moans drifted through the open window. The moans stabbed at her heart like millions of tiny pinpricks. Unable to bear the sound, she closed the bedroom window and replaced the blinds and curtains.

She retired to bed, slipping the 9mm under her pillow, and lit candles that were on the nightstand. She studied the painted roses in the warm yellow light—they appeared to dance in the candle-light as the shadows played tricks on her eyes.

"How wonderful it would be to be with you in the roses," she said.

Her eyes tired and dry, she removed her contacts and placed them in their storage case. She pulled a prescription bottle from the nightstand, took two, and blew out the light.

With a little help from her friend Valium, she slept—she dreamed of the roses.

The roses—red, vibrant, voluptuous—carried her away with their whispers. A heartbeat echoed in the distance. Slow and steady. She should be afraid, but she was not. Only peace and serenity were felt here. Supple petals caressed her skin as she melted into a soft cushion of grass and discarded petals. Petals danced on the breeze, floating through the air, creating their own mysterious ballet. They swirled, twirled, and danced around each other, never colliding—adrift with purpose. The soft petals kissed her cheeks, their heavenly scent embracing her and infusing itself into her skin and hair.

The heartbeat grew stronger as it neared. The rose bushes shivered in anticipation. Invisible hands parted the bushes, revealing nothing but black, empty space. But he's there—she could feel him. His strong presence peered at her from the void.

She's vulnerable and afraid. The dancing petals solidify into a crimson wall, placing a protective barrier between her and the black void. He whispered her name and the protective petals were vanquished as thorny vines restrained her. Her skin tingled with pain as the thorns stabbed into flesh. The voluptuous roses at the end of those vines shivered with laughter.

Again, he whispered her name.

She awoke, head buzzing with the scent of roses. Confused and half awake, she reached for Ryan but found the left side of the bed empty. Tears threatened suicide on the edges of her eyelids as reality regained its suffocating grasp.

Ryan was gone.

She was alone.

Sleep returned to her as she studied the walls in a nearsighted haze. Without her contacts or glasses, the roses were only bright-red, globulous shapes. They appeared to move across the plaster, as if floating in a soft breeze. She reached for her glasses on the nightstand. She turned back to the roses with clear vision and they were still—motionless.

Grief was slowly picking away at her sanity.

Ryan was dead. She couldn't accept it. At any moment, he was supposed to come home, kiss her on the forehead, and ask about her day. She held her breath and waited.

But he did not and would not ever come home again, kiss her on the forehead, or ask about her day.

She sighed.

The house was quiet with emptiness.

A succinct rumbled meow with a dash of purr tore her away from the roses. Mr. Kitty was sitting at the foot of the bed in a patch of yellow sunlight. His white fur was blinding to her sleep-tired eyes as he meowed again.

"I gotcha, kit cat," she said, dragging herself out of bed.

In a flash, Mr. Kitty ran to the kitchen as she slowly followed behind. Ryan remained at the door, moaning—desperate for that one little taste of living flesh.

She fed her beloved cat and returned to bed with another dose of her best friend—Valium.

She slept.

She returned to a bed of roses as petals rained down from above. The roses whispered at her ear as their petals caressed her bare arms. She opened her eyes and found she was no longer in the room where she slept. The day turned into the darkest night, illuminated only by starlight. Her bedroom was completely re-placed by a jungle of rose bushes six feet tall and without an end in sight. The full blooms weighed heavily upon their thorny stems as they swayed in the breeze.

Head clear of sleep and eyes wide open, this dream world was the most vivid she had ever experienced. She rose from the bed of roses. Her bare feet walked upon a warm soft carpet of grass. She took a deep breath as the fragrant air wrapped itself around her like a soft blanket.

She found herself in a clearing, the bushes towering over her. They shivered in anticipation. She began searching the edges of the clearing for a path, but none was found. One was seen out of the corner of her eye, but when she turned to look, there was nothing but more roses.

In the distance, she heard a heartbeat.

The tender breeze carried the familiar beat to her ear. She turned in circles, searching for the source. Despite the warm air, goose flesh erupted upon her skin.

The heartbeat grew stronger as it neared.

At the far side of the clearing, invisible hands parted the bushes, revealing nothing but black and empty space. But he's there, she can feel him. His strong presence peered at her from the void.

She took a step toward the void.

The heartbeat grew louder—stronger.

She stepped closer. As she reached the opening, the clearing erupted with a shower of petals, blocking the starlight. Within seconds, she was engulfed and suffocated by the petals. They clung to her skin, mouth, and nose. She couldn't breathe. Just as her mind lost consciousness, he laughed softly and whispered her name.

She awoke, her head buzzing with the maddening scent of roses. She reached for Ryan but found the left side of the bed empty. Anger swelled in her heart as her grief continued to pick away at her sanity. Mr. Kitty was at the end of the bed in his yellow sunspot, as he meowed his incessant rumbled meow.

"I get it, cat!" she yelled. "You're hungry!"

She grabbed the 9mm from beneath her pillow, threw the blanket back, and stomped out of the room. Mr. Kitty raced to the kitchen. She dumped food in his bowl as Ryan moaned at the door. She huffed her way to the door, the gun in hand with the safety off. She grabbed hold of the dead bolt as his moans resonated in the deepest parts of her heart.

Unable to open the door and destroy her zombified lover, she collapsed to the floor in tears. Mr. Kitty continued to eat his breakfast as she listened to Ryan's moans. It sounded like him. It had the same gravely tone as human Ryan did. The same tone she'd heard in her dreams as he whispered her name.

For hours she remained motionless on the floor listening to zombie Ryan's never ending misery. The gun in her hand weighed her down like an anchor. Each subsequent moan grew more sad and pathetic—lonely. Each moan killed a tiny part of her soul. Soon she would have nothing left. She played with the safety. On. Off. On.

Suddenly angry, she tore herself away from the cold vinyl floor and the pathetic zombified moans of her dead lover. She returned to the bedroom and ripped open the arsenal trunk, threw in the 9mm, and grabbed the AR-15.

Not caring how much noise she made, she ripped the curtains and blinds from the window. She opened the window and blindly fired into the backyard. Ten zombies immediately 'awakened,' their moans calling out to their brethren. Unable and unwilling to put a bullet in Ryan's head, she unleashed her grief and anger on the rest of them.

She opened fire and killed them all.

This time she refused her happy place. Her happy place with Ryan was dead and gone. Her soul was dying and she would do nothing to save it. Her happy place now was killing zombies and enjoying it. Their heads popped like blood-filled water balloons and she started to laugh.

Twenty more zombies came shuffling through the yard and she killed them all. She continued to shoot until the sun went down and she could no longer see. She reluctantly closed the window and returned to bed.

Two more Valium and the moans outside her window lulled her to sleep—she dreamt of the roses.

She awoke in the clearing. The petals continued their purposeful disarrayed ballet. She was calm and at peace here.

Mr. Kitty, his white fur tinted blue with starlight, ran about the clearing, chasing petals.

"I have to be hallucinating," she said.

At the sound of her voice, the cat stopped mid-stride and gave her a quizzical look. He blinked and let out a long bellowing meow.

"Come here, kit cat. What's the matter?"

He ignored her and ran around the clearing in circles, pouncing and clawing at the petals. The petals eluded his razor-sharp claws as they danced around him tauntingly. He growled in frustration.

She laid her head on a pillow of petals and gazed upon the stars. Millions of them glittered in the sky. The breeze carried the whisper of her name.

In the distance, the heartbeat began its approach. Not only did she hear it, she *felt* it. The rhythmic beat pulsed within her body— every nerve ending ebbing and flowing with the beat of his heart. She closed her eyes to the stars and relinquished herself.

Mr. Kitty growled from somewhere in the clearing. Her heartbeat matched his as a pleasured sigh escaped her lips. The rose bushes rustled as they parted.

Thorny vines restrained her, the air tinged with blood.

She felt his approach, and within seconds, his familiar touch. He slid his hand under her shirt, gently caressing her breasts, then ripped the shirt from her body. His lips grazed hers, gently at first—a small kiss. In unison, their heartbeats rose. He kissed her passionately deep as the thorns dug further into her flesh.

Oh, how I've missed the taste of you, she thought.

He released her from his kiss as his lips traced the line of her jaw, to her ear, and down her neck. Her skin tingled at his touch as their heart rates rose. She wanted to touch him, wrap her body around his, but the thorns kept her in place.

From somewhere in the clearing, Mr. Kitty growled and the kisses stopped. His heartbeat rapidly faded into the distance and grew silent. The thorny vines released her as silence overtook the clearing. She remained where she was—motionless, hoping he would come back.

"Give in," he whispered on the breeze.

Suddenly, Mr. Kitty jumped on her chest, dug his claws into her flesh, and growled as he hissed in her face.

She sprung from her bed, clutching the cat to her chest as he continued to hiss. She looked into his terrified face, his emerald eyes darting around the room, looking for the threat.

"Shhh, kitty," she said and stroked his head. "It's okay."

He stopped hissing and squirmed out of her grasp. She released him to the floor, his fur standing on end, puffed out like a blowfish as he ran from the room.

She looked around the room.

All seemed normal—except for the roses. She walked to the nearest wall and peered at them. They struggled against the plaster, trying to break free. She placed a fingertip to a painted petal, expecting to feel its velvety softness, but only felt smooth plaster.

On the first floor, at the far end of the house, Ryan's moans grew louder as he pounded on the kitchen door. She found Mr.

Kitty sitting at the back door, tauntingly meowing between Ryan's moans. After each meow, zombie-Ryan would bang on the door with renewed vigor.

"Bad kitty." She shooed the cat away. He strutted away with an evil-eyed look and sat beside his food bowl.

She reached for the deadbolt and turned it ever so slightly. Ryan slammed heavily into the door, shaking it in the frame. It was only a matter of time before he broke through. She returned the deadbolt to its full locked position. She fed Mr. Kitty and returned to the room where she slept.

In the upstairs hall, she smelled the roses. She stopped at the top of the stairs and inhaled a deep breath. She was high on the scent of her cherished flowers.

Not in the mood to kill zombies, she retreated to bed, and with the comforting guidance of her BFF Valium, she returned to the roses.

She stood in the clearing, the petals with a glint of starlight floating and swirling around her as the blooms continued to shiver in anticipation. Before her, the path was open and waiting. At the far end she saw Ryan. He stood with a hand reaching for her. He smiled a warm, inviting smile, as he had on their first date. In the distance, she could hear his heartbeat as a stream of swirling petals emanated from his core.

In time with the beat of his heart, the petals moved with purpose in her direction. Each beat carried the sound closer until finally it was all she heard and felt—like a thundering firework her chest vibrated with the boom of his heart as the petals crashed into her. The petals showered down around her as they fell into the stream that connected her to Ryan.

He whispered her name. "We can be happy here," he said.

She yearned to be with him. Every particle of her being, every particle of her soul wanted to run into his arms. She took a step forward and the path to her salvation disappeared. The petals dispersed into the air around her, as the connection between them was broken.

"Give in," he whispered. The words floated to her on the breeze and washed over her. Her yearning for him increased ten fold.

On the other side of the clearing, the rose bushes parted. She ran to the opening, the floating petals flurrying before her and blocking her view. She swatted them away. She saw Ryan at the end of the path. She ran to him, but he disappeared and the bushes enclosed their prison wall of leaves, rose blooms, and razor sharp branches around her.

"Give in," he whispered. A strong gust of wind knocked her off her feet as the floating petals formed dizzying patterns above her. Her yearning to be with him increased; now she knew what to do.

She awoke to the sound of trembling leaves. The roses trembled and quaked against their plaster prison—desperate to be free. Mr. Kitty sat in his sunspot at the end of the bed like an Egyptian Sphinx—a blood-red rose petal resting on the comforter between his front paws. He rumbled his typical meow.

Somewhere in the room, the plaster cracked, bits and pieces falling to the hardwood floor. The beckoning aroma of the roses slithered through the cracks as they continued to rage against their prison.

Again, Mr. Kitty meowed his rumbled meow.

She threw the covers back and headed for the kitchen. The cat quickly followed.

To the surprise of Mr. Kitty, she didn't feed him, but instead went directly to the kitchen door. Ryan's ever present moaning and door pounding continued, undeterred.

She reached for the wooden barricade across the door. Quietly, she removed it and leaned the two-by-four against the wall. The deadbolt clicked softly as it was removed from the latch.

She placed a hand on the doorknob and turned it.

The door opened and she stared into Ryan's decomposing face. The past few days had not been kind to him. Courtesy of Mr. Kitty and his claws, shredded pieces of flesh hung from his face as his skin slipped and separated from his skull.

His zombie stink washed over her like a suffocating tidal wave. She suppressed her gag reflex and breathed him in deeply. He stood in a small pool of black pus, and in that small pool of black pus next to Ryan's left foot, was Mr. Kitty.

Dead.

His body was eaten through to the spine, torn in two. His small ribcage poked through bits of torn flesh and plucked white fur. His left ear and side of his face were gone—ripped from the skull.

She looked to the cat food bowl and it was over flowing—not a single piece eaten. Her true reality broke through her Valium induced haze. She studied Ryan's decomposing face closer and spotted Mr. Kitty's white fur stuck to his lips and between his teeth. His white t-shirt and jeans were covered in the cat's blood.

She didn't think it possible that her heart could break anymore. As the remaining piece of her soul died, she shrugged off her brief moment of mental clarity and dove headfirst into insanity.

Instead of crumbling under the weight of her soul-crushing grief, she grabbed zombie-Ryan by his plain, no longer white t-shirt and pulled him into the house. She pushed him to the kitchen floor, then slammed the door closed, locked it, and replaced the wooden barricade.

Ryan moaned, as he lay on the floor, too stupid to turn over and lift himself up. As she walked past him, though, his supernatural hunger kicked in and he reached for her ankle. She evaded his sluggish grasp and he rolled onto his side. She walked backwards, keeping an eye on him as he rose to his knees. She took one step back and he had one foot on the floor. A second and third step back and Ryan was on his feet with arms outstretched, fingers hooked into claws as he prepared to launch his dead body towards the living-breathing flesh before him.

Before he could gain momentum, she turned and ran up the stairs, taking them two at a time. Ryan was close behind, no longer stupid as he tapped into the supernatural force that drove the undead.

Hunger.

His moans were no longer sad and pathetic, but eager and frenetic. He stomped up the stairs after her as the house shook with his chase.

Halfway up the stairs, she could smell the roses. No longer a beckoning aroma slithering through the cracked plaster, but a tether pulling her to the other side.

She reached the bedroom. Chunks of plaster were falling to the floor, as the roses broke free of their incarceration. The blooms quivered in excitement.

She stood beside the bed, out of breath. The rose infused air filled her lungs as Ryan's heavy footsteps stomped down the hallway. He reached the bedroom doorway as the ceiling above dissolved into the glittering starlit sky. He didn't break pace and she welcomed him with open arms as his putrescent body engulfed her.

Together they fell onto the bed, and as his teeth sank into her shoulder, the petals danced their disordered ballet above them.

The first bite took her breath away. She didn't struggle but instead wrapped herself around his body and gave into the pain. Ryan wrapped her in his arms, slid a hand along her neck, and grabbed a handful of her long dark brown hair. He jerked her head back, exposing her neck, and without hesitation, tore into her tender flesh with his teeth.

Pain.

Glorious, sweet, and agonizing pain rampaged through her body. Like a deep and painful hangnail being torn away, her skin ripped between his gnashing teeth. She tried to scream but her vocal cords, along with the rest of her throat, were between Ryan's teeth. Her blood, thick and warm, flowed to the nape of her neck, and soaked into the disheveled sheets below as her vision began to flicker.

In.

Zombie Ryan's visage, covered in blood, hovered inches from her face as he gnawed on her flesh. The smell of her own blood made her vomit. Stomach acid slithered into the wound left by Ryan's attack. The plaster walls of her bedroom continued to disintegrate as the roses pushed their way through—they shivered with laughter.

Out.

Nothing but blackness as his heartbeat began to beat in the distance. She could feel his presence in the void. A cool breeze rustled the leaves of the bushes as the petals' velvety softness caressed her skin. There was no pain here. Only serenity.

In.

Zombie-Ryan took another bite. His teeth scraped against her collarbone as her skin and tissue were removed. She heard an audible snap as muscle clung to bone in one last desperate attempt at salvation. Ryan grunted with a slight twitch of the jaw and the muscle was gone—torn from its home and masticated into nothingness. The bed dissolved underneath them and they were lying on a plush carpet of grass.

Out.

Small diamond pinpoints of light appeared in the blackness, as his heartbeat grew stronger. Her heart found his rhythm and they were in sync. The roses shivered with anticipation. Soon they would be together. The breeze carried the whisper of her name.

In.

With fingers interlaced in her long dark brown hair, Ryan pulled and her scalp began to tear. The skin separates and sloughs off like the skin of a snake. She wants to scream—needs to scream—through the pain. Unable to voice her agony, she endured in silence.

Out.

His heartbeat grew stronger still and every fiber of her being vibrated as her heart matched his cadence. In unison, their hearts danced as she relinquished herself to the slow and steady rhythm.

In.

Ryan released her to the carpet of grass and stood above her. In one smooth, quick motion, he plunged a hand into her chest. Bones cracked and broke as his fingers pierced like dull knives. Overrun by roses, the room where she slept vanished.

Out.

Together their hearts rose to a crescendo as he stood beside her. His fingers interlocked with hers and she was whole again.

In.

With both hands in her chest, zombie-Ryan grabbed hold of her ribcage—one hand on each side—as he pulled simultaneously in the opposite direction. Without hesitation, he dove head first into her chest cavity, grabbed hold of her still-beating heart with razor-sharp teeth, and ripped it from her chest.

Out.

She was standing in the clearing. The air was silent. Their heartbeats were still. Nothing moved. The roses were motionless and quiet. The stars glittered in the night sky. Before her, the rose bushes were parted like a stage curtain and she looked into her bedroom. The plaster walls were intact and free of protruding roses, her body on the bed being eaten by zombie-Ryan. The late afternoon sun filled the room and made the roses glow with a blood-red luminosity.

She watched from the clearing as zombie-Ryan swallowed the last piece of her heart. Her life extinguished, he simply stopped and remained on the bed, as he returned to his zombie stupor. Within minutes, her body reanimated and she was a member of the undead population. Her soul remained in the clearing, watching the end of her life like a movie.

She sighed as the curtain of roses fell and the room where she slept disappeared; her connection to the mortal world forever severed.

The petals rose from the clearing floor and continued their disarrayed ballet. From somewhere in the clearing, Mr. Kitty growled in frustration as the petals he chased tauntingly eluded him.

Ryan took hold of her hand, interlacing her fingers with his, and she reveled in the tingling sensation dancing upon her skin.

THE LOTTERY

CHAUMA SMITH GUS

Rick and Allen unchained the door to let me out. I picked up the pole and looked both ways as I stepped onto the sidewalk, breathing quietly through my mouth. The crowd had gathered to the left, no stragglers to the right. I heard the heavy door slam behind me, the chains rattling. I reached across and touched my MP3 player; as promised, it started playing immediately. It'd been so long I had to restrain the impulse to laugh out loud.

Instead, I walked into the street and waved my free hand at the crowd. "Hey! What're you doing over there? Lunch is this way!" The movement and noise caught their attention and they turned towards me in eerie unison. I waited a moment, watching their reactions, their shuffling steps moving faster against the broken asphalt. When most of them seemed like they were headed in my direction, I turned and jogged away briskly, the pole balanced and ready over my right shoulder. I counted my paces in threes, it helped me keep the rhythm for the grand finale.

The morning was sunny, which meant the pavement was dry and my footing was good. Oil still oozed from the street when it rained; those were the runs that just sucked. As warm as the sun was on my face, the hot springtime weather brought out the stink from the dead things wandering the streets.

I turned right onto Tenth Avenue, scanning the shadows and sidewalks for more shamblers. I hollered again at the few I passed; they turned and started to follow, reaching for me.

See, back before 'It Happened,' I thought I was a zombie buff. I'd seen the movies, read the books, read the survival guides, knew my stuff. I always wondered what the big deal was with the slow ones—after all, if you're quick on your feet, you can run away, right? Problem is, you have to rest. They don't.

The good news is Pete had read all the books I'd missed, and all the stuff on the internet. Pete's the one who came up with the lemming game. The way he told it, folks would send a dog up onto a rooftop or the edge of a cliff, and it would bark until the shamblers came to get lunch. Then the dog would lead them to the edge, and they would all crowd the edge until most of them fell off and got smashed on the ground below. That's fine, we said, but we don't have a cliff, and we don't have a dog.

"Don't need a cliff when you have an eight story parking garage. Don't need a dog when you have a track and field team." Pete looked at us, twelve kids on a visiting JV track team, our uniforms ragged, our coach and chaperones all dead.

Great.

I flipped a bird at a dead woman as she lunged at me, a guy in a torn-up business suit knocking her over as he tried to get to me as I skimmed past. No big deal, I could run away. The pole flexed a little with the motion of my jog. My pace was steady. I could do ten miles at this pace and they wouldn't catch me. I'd win the lottery again.

I've won the lottery more times than I want to think about. There's two ways to do it, now. The first is to pull a long straw when it's time to go running, and the second is to survive the run. This morning wasn't any different than any other running day.

The moaning was getting loud again. We didn't really even have to talk about it, any more; we just got dressed in the morning and thought about what we'd rather have for breakfast. This week it was mostly cold beans. With that out of the way, we climbed up to the roof. Pete supervised, as usual, even though he was too old and too slow.

"Ready?" We gathered around Rick, our captain; he held out a purple felt fedora filled with dominoes, of all things. "Snake eyes wins," he said. He held up the piece in question, a pair of dots on one side. He dropped it in and stirred them around. I don't know why he feels the need to change the game every time. Short straw, black pebble, scrap of paper with an 'X' or a red dot or something else equally silly. He used to try to explain where each game came from, till Ava finally yelled at him—we don't care. It's not a secret that Rick thinks he loves her, or at least wants to get in her pants, so we weren't surprised that he shut up about it. But he continued to make up new games of chance to distract us from what we were really doing. The winner gets whatever they want after they come back from the run, as long as it was available.

We all reached in, picked up a piece and held our fists closed until all twelve of us had drawn. Rick pulled last, then put the fedora down. We opened our hands at the same time, and I stared at the 'winning' piece in my palm.

"Anything I want, right?" I asked. They all nodded. I pulled my MP3 player out of my pocket and held it out to Pete, the charger cable looping out of my fingers.

"Charge it when you turn on the generator tonight. I won't run till tomorrow morning, when I have my tunes to run with."

Pete looked thoughtful, then nodded, looking at my hand, not my face. "We can wait until tomorrow, sure." He took the player carefully. I kept the ear buds in my pocket and turned to go back inside, pretending not to notice that no one would meet my glance.

That's the way it was—no one would look the bait in the eye until it was over. The rest were too ashamed it wasn't them.

There are sixty or so of us left, we think, at least on Southside. We live huddled on the top floors of an old hotel, and the two most dangerous 'jobs' in the world are going shopping and playing bait when it's time to move the crowds of shamblers in the streets. Good thing our team was in town early for a regional meet when things went to hell; otherwise everyone else would starve or feed the shamblers. Good for the adults, that is—they were all slower, so of course they were exempt from duty as bait. We run, they go shopping, just like the old days.

The first music track ended, then went to the next one, and I grinned. 'Camel Walk' may be old, and it had dumb lyrics, but it had mostly the same beat as my distance pace, so it was perfect. God, I miss Captains' Wafers.

I dodged another group, glancing over my shoulder as I turned onto Twelfth Ave. Easy breezy, maybe thirty ghouls behind me. If there was going to be a problem, it would be up ahead, after I turned onto Fifteenth Ave. The church fountain at Five Points attracted more shamblers than a school bus full of fifth graders, and I had quite a fan club already.

So the deal was, the 'winner' gets to go be bait, and if they make it, they get whatever they want. I think if Rick ever gets to go, he'll ask Ava to spend the night with him, and I'm pretty sure she'll agree, just on principle. What's funny about that is Shorty and I have made the run more times than anyone else. Rick never goes, Ava never goes, the rest have gone a time or two, but I've been out twelve times, and Shorty's been out at least ten. Apparently, Rick doesn't want to get laid badly enough to risk dying.

That's okay. It's random and supervised by Pete, so it's fair. Right? At least I know I've got my tunes, even if it will only last for a few hours.

I rounded the corner at Fifteenth and wished I hadn't eaten. I didn't puke, didn't have time to puke. A line of shamblers was ahead of me, already walking my way. I adjusted my grip on my pole, scanning for something to anchor on. Thankfully, the streets were in poor repair even before 'It Happened.'

A pothole presented itself a yard or two in front of the advancing line of walkers. I took a short sprint, (one—two—three!) planted myself and vaulted over the line, going a little for height, a little for distance, keeping my grip on my pole as my body arced over and I flew through space. No mat for this competition. I landed rough and tried to shoulder roll out of it. The pole hit the ground hard, but there's never time to think about that in this race. My shoulder and knees got skinned, but I was back up and back running, rebalancing my precious fiberglass vaulting pole over my shoulder. Three meters in front, three meters behind, leading the way for my feet. Cue 'oohs' and 'ahhhs' from the crowd, except this crowd was disappointed that I'd recovered. They smelled my blood as it started running down my arm and legs.

Past the fountain, my fan club was up to about fifty now— more than enough. "Going up!" I shouted to the living human watchers on the roof. I turned into the parking garage, and settled back into my slower distance pace. If I lost too many of them, it would all have to be done again sooner, and I didn't want to even look at another domino for a while, even for a few precious hours of music.

'Camel Walk' finished, and the random shuffle brought up 'Put a Ring On It'. At least it had a beat, at least it wasn't fifteen years old, and it was a better match for my pace, bright and bouncy, and unconcerned by zombies.

I don't care how many times I've done it, the parking garage always creeps me out. I have nightmares about it even when I don't have to run.

I'd moved most of the cars, one by one, till there was a way that was mostly clear of blind spots on the straight-aways. The corners were dark and spooky, and the ceilings aren't high enough to vault over anything coming down the ramps at me. Something moved on the next level. I caught the motion out of the corner of my eye through the cable barrier dividing the sloping levels. It was fast, maybe a cat. I kept up my pace, rounding onto the third ramp. Sixteen total, eight floors of parking, and uphill all the way till the last sprint.

I could hear the shamblers behind me, probably trailing by the full length of the building. I slowed a bit more to let them catch up a little. They were more excited than usual, probably from the trail of sweat and blood I was leaving. Three quarters, two thirds, they came and I let them. My stomach clenched but I kept my breathing under control—if I panicked, I would die, game over.

When they were half a deck behind me, I picked up the pace again, rounding the corner of 5 and glancing up the ramp of 6. A flicker of movement again in the shadows, fast and running away from me, and rounding onto 7. It was too big to be a cat.

Something was up ahead of me, above me. I didn't know how far. Then it shrieked, loud. I stumbled when I heard it. My fans got more excited and picked up speed till there was only a third of the ramp behind me still clear. Shamblers don't make that kind of noise, nothing I've seen in weeks moves that fast. Oh God. Please let me get to the last jump, Mom, I'm sorry. You were right all along.

I lost my rhythm, and Beyonce's beat was faster than my feet.

"Shut up, shut up, go, go, go, can't stop now, can't stop now." My voice was breathy and low, but it steadied me. My feet found the ground, my breath was the wind behind me. Screw the game, it was time to go. I picked up the pace, thumbing up the volume on my player. Then I was back, pulling ahead again. Level 7, level 9, I was three quarters ahead, but they weren't stopping, weren't slowing. Around 10, then 11, then 12. Another shriek, but it was going away from me. Away was good. I began to breathe easier. I rounded 13, 14, and 15. I could see the sunlight falling on the last turn.

It was bright enough to make me squint as I made my way out of the hellish darkness of moans and the stench of decay. I always thought about that story I'd read in English, from Greek mythology, about the guy who came out of the underworld. I never could remember his name.

The roof of the eighth floor should be clear to the railing. One hundred and sixteen paces, jump, then the flight from there to the next rooftop. Then to the mat made out of boxes and mattresses. I was almost there, almost there…

The zombie in front of me shouldn't have been there. It shouldn't move that way. It was crossing my path, way too fast. But I could be faster; fifty paces and I could go around it.

This one was different. It would need a new name. What do we call it? It's not a shambler. It looks different.

I needed to shut up and run, think of the angle when I jump. If I twisted a little, I would be able to straighten out…

The zombie stank, as it reached for me, but I ran past as its fingers ripped the MP3 player from my waist. The ear buds were yanked away. It grabbed at my pole and jerked, but I jerked back and reached for the edge of the railing with the leading end. The place where it was marked for me.

There was sweat in my eyes, blood on my skin, one—two—three—sailing through space and I look down, looked for the ground, where I would land on the building, arching my body and twisting a little.

Rick was yelling; they were shoving the mat to the left. Allen backed up a pace and charged as I came down, using his own body to slam me to the mat. My roll was sloppy and I heard something break inside me, but I was down, I was alive.

Behind me, across the street on top of the parking garage, the thing shrieked at us. My fan club came up behind it, shambling and reaching for me across the distance, pushing and shoving, and then falling off the edge, carrying the thing down with them.

If I had anything clever to say, I would do it now, but the run was over, and the sound of bodies smashing into the pavement always made me puke.

It's over, I'm done. I lost my MPs.

The music is gone forever.

AWAKENING EVIL

JENNIFER GORACZKOWSKI

"Sydney, I'm over here," Sadie called from a lonely booth in the back of the restaurant, while waving her hand toward her sister.

"Sorry I'm late. Some kid spilled soda down my pants so I had to change." I threw my bag next to Sadie and slid into the booth. "So, what have you figured out?"

"I ordered a couple of appetizers, but I can get more if you're hungry."

"No, I'm not that hungry." What I really wanted was Sadie's plan for taking on the local wolf pack. "Are we going to talk or not."

"We have time, so relax." Sadie took a drink and sat back.

For twins, we couldn't be more different. First of all, I was blonde and my sister was a brunette. Second, she was all about action and was very impulsive. Me, I like to look at the big picture before I act. The most important difference; she's a wolf and I'm a necromancer.

"You look like you have a lot on your mind. What's wrong?" Sadie asked.

"Nothing, I was just thinking."

The waitress placed the three appetizers on the table. "Is there anything else?" she asked.

"No," Sadie said while I shook my head. "Here, have a plate."

I took it, placing it in front of me. "I can't eat until I know what's going on."

"Stop being a baby. You know everything will be fine. I always have a plan."

"That's the problem, it's *your* plan. I'm never included. I'd feel better if we discussed it before we ate."

"Fine. Where do you want me to start?"

"Just tell me this plan of yours." I leaned back and folded my arms across my chest.

"I found out that Colorado's alpha is out of state and should be gone for a while. So, we shouldn't have much resistance from the pack. They'll be lost without him giving orders."

If what she said was true, this would be easier than either one of us had anticipated. "How long will he be gone?"

"For a while." She stuffed a French fry in her mouth. "I guess there were some problems with a pack out of state and he's there helping them."

"That sounds fishy to me. Who do you find these things out from?"

"It doesn't matter, but it's the truth."

I leaned into the table and placed my elbows on it. "That still doesn't tell me how we're going to take over."

"Don't you see? With the alpha gone, that gives me the opportunity to challenge his position. Since he isn't here to defend himself, I'll take back what's ours."

I sighed. "And where does that leave me? I'm not a wolf and I have no place in this pack."

"Sydney, you're my only family and will always have a place in the pack."

She always says that to me, but somehow I knew I'd be left to defend myself once she was surrounded with people like her.

"Plus, how else would we be able to take over the pack without the help of an army?" She picked up her glass and took a long drink.

"An army?" I hesitated. "You're not suggesting…" I stopped from finishing my statement.

Sadie nodded. "Yes I am."

"I can't do it." Over the last few years, I've had to learn to control my emotions, because when I lose control, dead things start showing up on my doorstep, and opening my front door to a rotting corpse was not a very good way to start the day.

Sadie reached across the table and took hold of my hands. "I know you can do it, sis. You've gotten so much better at controlling those things, and with a dozen or so of them on our side we can…"

I cut in. "First of all, those things, they're people, and somebody's loved one. Calling them to do my dirty work is horrible. You've seen how the bodies are returned when I'm done with them. They're always missing body parts and their skin seems to melt away after I've had them for a few days."

"Sydney, your ability is a gift. Embrace it and use it."

There was no arguing with Sadie, I always gave in to her, and this time would be the same. I would call the dead to help her take over the pack and she would become their new alpha, like she'd dreamed about.

"What's wrong?" Sadie asked.

"You need me to reanimate dozens of bodies." I hesitated and took a deep breath. "The last time I did that, everyone died."

"You're older now, and you've had a lot more practice."

"I suppose."

"You don't look happy. Why don't we eat and we can talk about this a little more later."

I nodded and watched as Sadie filled her plate.

She could act as if everything would work out perfectly, but I was worried and I began to think about the first time I realized I could call the dead.

I'd only been sixteen.

"Mom, we're home!" Sadie dropped her bag by the door and went into the kitchen.

I followed a few steps behind her. "Where's Dad?"

"He's still working, but should be home for dinner," Mom said as she turned around and handed us cookies. "Speaking of dinner, have you two decided where you want to go for your sixteenth birthday yet?"

"Can't we just stay home?" I asked.

"That's no fun," Sadie said. "I want to go out for pizza."

"Why do you want to stay here for your birthday?" Mom asked.

Sadie looked at me and raised her eyebrows.

"Never mind, pizza sounds good." I tried to smile as I said it and Mom didn't push the topic. "Well, I'm going to do my homework. I'll be in my room," I said.

Before I could close the door, Sadie was following me in. "Why do you always have to be the party pooper?"

"This town sucks. We live in the middle of nowhere and these people hate us here. Why would I want to go out to eat with them?"

"Maybe we can talk them into taking us to the city for our birthday."

"Sadie, we've tried that every year for as long as I can remember and we're always told we need to stay out of the big cities for our safety. What makes you think this year will be any different?"

"It was just a thought. You don't have to get upset."

"I'm not upset."

The front door opened.

"Dad's home," Sadie said as she raced to the front door.

It slammed quickly and the windows in my room shook. I wanted to see what was wrong so I went to the kitchen and stood in the doorway. Mom was working on dinner, Sadie was at the table, and Dad was washing his hands.

"What happened?" Mom asked.

"When I got to my car the front tires were flat," he said.

"Both of them?"

"Yep. They looked like they were slashed."

"Who would do that?"

"Do you really have to ask me that? You know the people in this town."

Mom cleared her throat and looked in our direction.

"Sorry, girls. This is a discussion your mom and I should have a little later," Dad said.

I went to stand next to Sadie. "We're almost sixteen now. You can talk around us," I said.

"Yeah, it's not like we don't know what you say when you're in your room. I can always hear you two," Sadie added.

"Well, this topic is one you don't need to hear." Dad reached into his pocket and pulled out a five dollar bill. "Why don't you and your sister go down to the corner store and get a gallon of milk." He handed the bill to me.

"Fine," Sadie said as she stood up. "Let's go."

We walked out of the house, and could hear them start discussing everything that had happened today.

"I wish they'd stop treating us like kids."

"I know, but I don't mind sometimes." I kicked a pebble on the ground. "It's better than listening to them argue."

It took Sadie and me twenty minutes to reach the corner store. When we got there, Mr. Mitchell was sitting in the same chair in the front of his store. He'd been there every day since we started coming here. He was the only person in this town that was polite to us.

"Ladies," he said and tipped his cowboy hat. "How can I help ya'll today?"

"We need some milk," I said as I tucked my hair behind my ears.

"Ya know where it's at." He pointed into the store. "Help yourselves."

We both walked in. I laid the money on the counter and Sadie took the milk from the glass-doored refrigerator wall unit.

"Thanks, Mr. Mitchell," I said as we left the store.

"You're welcome," he smiled, lowering the hat over his eyes once more.

Sadie and I started the walk back home. There was a siren in the distance, and I could see smoke coming from the direction of our house.

"Do you see that, Sydney?" she asked me.

"Yes."

"Do you think…" She stopped her question and started to run, dropping the milk on the ground.

We both ran as fast as we could, but Sadie beat me up the hill. I approached her as she stood looking at our house.

"Oh my God!" Sadie cried.

Our house was engulfed in flames and the black smoke was billowing up as far as I could see.

We started running. "Hurry up!" Sadie called.

As we reached the house, the front windows exploded and glass sprayed us. Every way in was blocked. The flames were too much.

"Mom!" I screamed.

Sadie ran around the back of the house and then rejoined me. "Did you seen them come out?"

I shook my head and began to cry. Sadie wrapped her arms around me and joined in the crying. The sound of sirens were approaching; help was finally arriving. Once the firefighters started to put out the flames, there wasn't much left of the house. The charred frame that was our home was the only thing left standing.

"Can you tell me what happened here?" Sheriff Wells asked.

We both shook our heads.

"Have you found our parents yet?" I asked.

"Yes, but it's best we remove their remains once the building is safe to enter."

There was no sensitivity in his tone. He actually sounded happy they were gone, and that really upset me. "Those are our parents you're talking about. Are you saying both of them died in there?" I said.

"Yep. Do you two have any family that can come get you?"

"No, sir," Sadie said.

"Then you'll need to come with me and I'll find a place for you stay for the night. Tomorrow I'll call Social Services and they can come get you."

I looked at Sadie and she wrapped her arms around me again.

"I'm going to ask you both one more time; do you know what happened here?"

"We already told you no," Sadie snapped at the sheriff.

"Now listen here, young lady, I'm just trying to find out what happened."

"No you're not. You're blaming us," I said.

"How were you able to escape the fire?" he asked.

Mr. Mitchell walked up behind the sheriff and said, "They weren't here."

"How do you know that?" Wells asked.

"They were at my store buyin' milk when this happened." He opened his arms to me and my sister. "You ladies are more than welcome to stay with me tonight."

"I have more questions for them, so I'll be taking them in for the night," Wells said.

I'm not sure if it was the sheriff's lack of concern or the fact that he thought we were responsible for the fire that set Sadie off, but she started to breathe heavy and her body began to shake uncontrollably.

"Sadie, what's happening to you?" My heart was racing and I thought I was going to lose her, too.

The sheriff backed away as Sadie fell to the ground, her body still shaking. When her eyes rolled to the back of her head, I had to back away, too, running into Mr. Mitchell.

"Don't worry, this is perfectly normal the first time," he said, whispering into my ear.

"The first time?" I questioned as I turned to face him.

He nodded and adjusted the hat on his head, "Ya'll had to know it was comin'. Didn't your parents warn ya?"

"Warn us about what?" He had me completely confused. We'd never been told about seizures or experienced anything like them in our family before. He sounded like he knew what was happening so he was who I turned to for answers. "Please, Mr. Mitchell what's happening to her?"

He knelt next to Sadie. "Young lady, I need ya to focus and stop fightin' the process. It'll be much easier that way."

"Please help…" I started to say as I turned to the sheriff, but he was gone and there was a trail of dust leading down the street.

The fire truck followed a moment later. They all left us, my sister and I only had Mr. Mitchell now.

As I started to cry, I went to my sister's side. Mr. Mitchell held her hand and the convulsions seemed to be stopping.

"Is she okay now?" I asked.

"The process is just startin'; she still has the hard part ahead of her."

"The hard part?"

"Never mind that now, let's get her somewhere safe where no one can see her."

I saw what he meant. There were still several onlookers around us who had come out to see the fire. We picked Sadie up under her arms and carried her down the street and used a van to cover us from prying eyes.

As we set her down, Sadie's body began to change. The bones in her arms and legs began to crack and become deformed. They were twisting and becoming longer. Her back arched and she rolled over to all fours. Her clothes began to rip from her body and small dark hairs began to cover her body. She looked up toward me and her eyes moved to the side of her face. Her nose darkened and became elongated.

I stumbled backwards and landed on the ground. "What's going on?" I screamed as I tried to crawl away.

Standing before me was a dark wolf with bright blue eyes. Much larger than any animal I'd ever seen before. If I hadn't witnessed the process, I wouldn't have believed that this was my sister.

Sadie took a step toward me and I tried to back away from her. "Leave me alone. Don't come any closer."

"She's just in shock. Why don't you head to the hills and run off some of your energy. You can meet us at my place later tonight," he told my sister.

Sadie turned and disappeared behind a nearby house. A few seconds later, a howl could he heard in the distance.

"Let's go. I'll make ya somethin' to eat and you can get some rest."

Mr. Mitchell offered me his hand and I stood up. "Will she be okay?"

He nodded.

First my parents and now my sister, my life was ruined. I lifted my hands to cover my eyes and began to sob. "What am I going to do now? Why is this happening to us?"

"Your sister was born that way." We started to walk down the driveway. "I just don't understand how ya didn't know. Your parents should've explained these things to ya a long time ago."

"Can you tell me what's going on?"

Mr. Mitchell nodded. The entire walk was filled with explanations of who we are and why we were living in this small town in Arizona. I learned more about my life in that twenty minute walk than in sixteen years of living with my parents. It turned out that my sister was a werewolf and I was not. The news was easy to take, because after watching what she went through to change, I never wanted to do that.

Mr. Mitchell also told me that my parents had to move to this town after they got married because he was a wolf and she was a witch. His pack didn't want them be together because she was too powerful, since my sister was a wolf like my dad, than maybe I was a witch like my mom. The only problem was that I could never remember any strange things happening to me like Sadie. So, I was doubtful.

Mr. Mitchell had a house right behind the store. He unlocked the back door and let me in first. "Why don't ya get cleaned up and I'll get ya somethin' to eat."

I walked into the bathroom, closed the door and sat on the toilet. If my sister ever came back, we were in trouble. Mr. Mitchell said we could stay with him for a few days, but he didn't want to draw too much attention to himself, so we would have to move on. Like my family, he was here to avoid trouble. He was also a wolf that had stirred up problems in his prior life. What were we going to do? The best thing right now, was to eat and get some rest. Maybe tomorrow Sadie would come back and we could talk about it. As I started to turn the water on in the sink, I heard someone pounding on the front door. If that sheriff was coming to take me, I wasn't going with him. I don't care how, but I would run away before that happened.

As I left the bathroom to investigate, there was another bang against the door. "Mr. Mitchell, would you like me to get that?"

There was no answer.

"Mr. Mitchell? Are you in the kitchen?"

When he didn't answer the second time, I went and opened the front door.

The person standing there was like a creature from my worst nightmare. He was a large man, wearing a torn-up leather jacket and black leather chaps over a pair of jeans. One foot still had a boot covering it, but the other one was missing and the flesh that should have been covering the foot was gone, along with most of the toes.

The skin that wasn't covered in dried blood was pale and had very little color. I could only see one of his murky white eyes because the bandana he was wearing was covering half of his face. The side I could see was raw from his chin, up to the top of his head. His bottom lip was torn so badly that it was hanging freely and his entire bottom set of teeth were exposed, well, the ones that he had left. One arm was broken and the ulna bone was completely exposed; it jutted through the skin.

I screamed and tried to close the door, but he was already coming in and reaching for me. There was a chair close to the door, and since I was in a hurry to get away from this monster, I tripped over it and landed flat on the floor. He continued into the house, dragging his broken foot behind him and moaning like he was in pain.

"MR. MITCHELL!" I screamed as I tried to scurry backwards to get away.

The back door slammed closed. "Why did you let it in?" Mr. Mitchell asked as he swung a wooden baseball bat at the man's head.

The bat connected with his chin and sent the bottom jaw flying, but he didn't stop coming. So Mr. Mitchell swung the bat one more time, this time in a chopping motion, coming straight down on the man's head. As soon as there was contact, the pressure caused the skull to shatter, sending shards of bone and brain matter in all directions. The body fell to the floor and didn't get back up. As it lay there, a dark oozing liquid began to drain from the head, pooling around the body.

The rancid smell caused me to gag and that quickly turned to full on vomiting. I didn't bother trying for the bathroom; I just let it out where I was sitting on the floor.

"Once you're finished, we need to talk about this." He didn't stand there watching or waiting for me, but disappeared around the corner and into the kitchen.

When I joined him, he was sitting on the back step, looking out to the hills behind his house.

"All done?" he asked without turning to look at me.

"Yes," I said, unsure if the vomiting truly was finished.

"Why don't we head out back to talk." He stood up and walked down the three steps.

I joined him quickly because I didn't want to be left in the house alone. "What was that thing in there?"

"That's what you would call the living dead."

"Huh?" I hesitated. "What're you saying? How can you be so calm about all of this?" I was so confused I didn't know what to ask or do anymore. I pointed back to the house. "That man, or *thing*, he was trying to get me."

"They're also called walkers or zombies."

"That was a *zombie*? Aren't those just in the movies?"

"After seein' your sister, are ya really gonna ask me that?"

That was a good point, but really, a zombie? "How did it get here and what did it want?"

"I don't know. You called him here."

"No, I didn't."

"You must have some of your mom in ya after all." He stopped and turned to face me. "That man was killed this mornin' while ridin' his motorcycle through town. He lost control of his bike and…" He stopped with the details. "Well, he ended up here after you called him. His body was bein' kept at the hospital morgue. Now, as far as I know, that was the only recent dead body in town so, we shouldn't have to worry about any more showin' up."

I dropped to my knees and started crying. "I'm sorry, I didn't mean to. Please tell me how to stop it from happening again."

Mr. Mitchell came to my side and placed a hand on my shoulder, "Unfortunately, I can't do that."

"What's happening to me?"

"You're what's called a Necromancer. That's a person who can communicate with, raise, and command the dead." He knelt next me. "You're a very rare person. The last necromancer I heard of died in the sixties and we haven't seen another once since."

I wiped the tears away. "Do you have any more information?"

"Very little. But I do know that ya need to be careful. Until a body has entered the ground, you can control it. They'll come when ya call 'em and won't stop till they find ya."

"So that thing in there wasn't trying to eat me?"

"No, but if ya call more than ya can control, they'll do as they please. That means killin' and eatin'."

How could I learn to control myself if I didn't know how to turn it on and off? I wished my mom was here, she'd know what to do.

"I'm gonna head in and clean the place up. Why don't ya stay out here for a bit."

What else was I going to do? I just nodded while staring at the ground.

Sadie was off running through the hills, and I was stuck here with a dead body, one that somehow I summoned to me. No matter how I looked at it, this was a curse. I didn't want to surround myself with dead people, especially ones that I had no idea how to control. I needed to figure out how I called the man, so I could make sure not to do it again. If he was the only dead body in town, then I needed to go somewhere I could find more.

While I sat there staring at the sun setting in the distance, Mr. Mitchell came out a few times carrying plastic bags to the trash. He would look at me, but wouldn't say anything, just continued with his business.

My legs were bent under the weight of my body for so long that they fell asleep. I had to get up and stretch them out. Since it was going to be dark soon, I walked to the street and looked out over the small town. Sadie had to be out there somewhere, hopefully staying safe and not causing any trouble. Every person in town carried a gun and I could only imagine how they would react to a large wolf wandering around. As I turned to head in, I could see movement in the distance, maybe a mile or so away. It looked like a small mob of people were coming this way.

Since they were walking through open desert, my heart skipped a beat. What if they were more dead bodies coming because I called them? I rushed back into the house. "Mr. Mitchell we may have a problem."

He didn't say anything, just followed me out to the street.

"Can you see them?" I pointed to the group that appeared to be getting larger. "They're moving pretty fast. Do you think they're…" I stopped because I felt awkward saying it out loud.

"Sydney, I need ya to think real hard. What did ya do to call them? The next town isn't for miles, so if you're strong enough to call them this far, then we may have a big problem if ya can't control them."

I shook my head. "I don't know what I did or how to stop them. Do you really think I'm the one who called them?"

He tilted his hat and wiped his brow. "I know you're the one who did." He turned toward the house and I followed. "They'll be here soon."

"What should I do?"

"Watch them and let me know when they're here."

Mr. Mitchell went from room to room, obviously looking for something that he couldn't find. Each time he came back to me, he was empty handed. Finally, he stopped and joined me at the window.

"Here's what's gonna happen. They're comin' to you." He saw my expression change to fear. "Don't worry, they shouldn't hurt ya if ya stay calm. They need you to tell 'em what to do."

"But I don't know…"

"Stop talkin' like that," he cut me off. "You have to figure it out."

"And if I can't?"

"Then we're all in trouble."

"What will happen?"

"Remember how I told ya about the last necromancer?"

I nodded.

"Well, he wasn't a very nice fella. He used the dead as a weapon. But he called too many and lost control of 'em."

"What did they do?"

"Their basic instincts took over and they killed a lot of people."

I had to swallow hard, if I wasn't able to figure something out soon, I was going to be responsible for the killing that these things were going to do.

"I want ya to know that I'll do my best to help ya, but if they start comin' after me, I have to go."

"Go where?"

"Far away from here. Those creatures can consume a grown man in a matter of minutes."

"Consume?" Once I questioned him, I realized what he was saying. "You mean *eat*?"

"Yep," he said as he was nodding.

"That's what they do? They eat people?"

"Enough talkin' about what they can do. They're gettin' pretty close. Try to command them, make them do somthin'."

I looked out at the group, counting fifteen. All had torn clothes and were in different levels of decay. A few were moving faster than the rest and I could only assume that was because there wasn't as much wrong with their bodies.

The ones in the back had missing body parts or were dragging broken legs behind them. I shuddered when I realized the person in front was missing the top portion of her forehead; it looked like it had been blown away.

"Are ya tryin' to stop them? Because it ain't workin' if you are," Mr. Mitchell said as he put his hand on my shoulder.

I was so busy looking at them, I forgot I was suppose to be trying to stop them. I began to shake my head. "I can't. I don't think I can do this. I've never even seen a dead body until today and now you're asking me to control an entire group of them?"

Backing away from the window, Mr. Mitchell took hold of my shoulders. "Ya have to do this, there's no choice."

He was asking me to do something I knew I couldn't. I wasn't strong like my sister was.

"Sydney, do somethin'," he ordered.

By now, the front of the house was full of zombies trying to get to me. They were banging on the windows and pounding on the front door. Luckily, the windows were set high and they could barely reach them, otherwise they would have broken in easily.

"Stop!" I screamed at the door.

For a breath, the noise stopped, but then started back up again.

"It didn't work, now what?"

"Ya have to do more than yell at 'em. They need to finish whatever it is that ya called 'em for."

"That's a problem because I don't know why they're here!" I sat on the floor and wrapped my arms around my body, beginning to cry as I rocked from side to side. I knew it was only a matter of time before they figured out how to get in, but I was hoping it would take a little bit longer. Unfortunately, one of the windows shattered and the zombies started crawling over each other to reach it.

Mr. Mitchell knelt in front of me. "I'm gonna head out back. I can keep an eye on ya, and if ya really need me, I'll be here."

"No, please don't leave me."

"It's not safe for me to be in here, there's just too many of 'em. Remember, they won't hurt ya. You're controlling them." He ran into the kitchen, the back door slamming closed as he left.

I was alone, well sort of. I still had dead people climbing through a window to get at me, but that wasn't comforting.

I stood up and ran into the kitchen, and as I reached for the back door handle, I paused. These were people and I was the reason they couldn't be laid to rest. My guilt got the best of me and I turned around.

The woman leading the group was the only one that made it into the house so far.

She was missing most of her forehead and had blood running down each side of her face. One eye was swollen shut and the other was staring directly at me, looking to me for the peace she desired.

That wouldn't happen until I let her go.

She stopped inches from me and I cringed, squeezing my eyes closed. I still couldn't help feeling she was there to hurt me.

Slowly, one eye at a time, I opened them. She was just standing there, and I knew she needed something I didn't know how to provide. Scanning her body, I saw her bodily fluids pooling around her feet.

The odor of decay and rot filled the kitchen as other zombies joined us. Some were not as steady on their feet and they fell over and ran into each other. The pile of bodies was growing and they began tearing and biting at one another.

"Stop!" I ordered, trying to sound as if I was in command of the group. "Stand up."

One at a time, the pile grew smaller as each stood up the best they could. By the time they were standing, I was able to see there was one body still on the floor. It was a man. Both of his legs had been broken in the commotion.

The rest of the group looked around the room and snarled occasionally as they gazed at each other. My heart was pounding. I didn't know what to do next. Why did I call them?

I replayed today's events in my mind. The fire and my parents were the first thing I thought about. Tears formed and I covered my eyes.

As I did, the snarling grew louder. Looking at the group, they were pulling and tearing at each other again.

"Stop!" I realized at that moment that whatever emotion I showed would set them off. Getting emotional caused me to lose focus and my control. But I still didn't have the answer I needed. Why were they here?

Then I remembered what happened to my sister and the sheriff taking off, leaving me. How could he do that? Shouldn't he have taken me to Social Services as an orphan? And before leaving, he'd tried to blame me and my sister for the fire.

I looked the dead woman right in the face, and for a brief moment, she looked as if she was smiling.

I had to look again. Her blood-filled mouth actually was grinning. Then she turned and made her way through the crowd of remaining zombies.

Did I just give her instructions? Her purpose for being here? The rest of the group was still looking at me, awaiting orders. What do I tell them?

My entire life I was the one that took a back seat to my sister. She could hear things, run faster, and I accepted that she was better than me. Today, I learned I had power. A power much better than running fast or changing into a wolf. I felt good, strong and confident. This town held my family down and they needed to pay and I finally had the power to make them.

I stood at the back door of Mr. Mitchell's kitchen and watched as every zombie turned and left his house. A plan had been set in motion and I was the creator.

I ran to the front of the house to watch as my work made their way in separate directions toward the center of town.

The back door opened and I went to the kitchen.

"Ya figured it out. I'm proud of ya," Mr. Mitchell said. "Did ya send them back?"

I shook my head. "Nope. I'm not sending them back until they finish what I've sent them to do."

"What did ya do?" he asked.

"Where's your mop so I can clean this mess up?" I asked ignoring his question.

He grabbed my shoulders and pulled me close. "Sydney, what did ya do?"

I stepped back and out of his grip. "I did what my parents couldn't do. I'm standing up to this town and showing them that they've destroyed the wrong family."

"You've sent 'em to town?"

I nodded, feeling pretty proud of myself.

"They're gonna kill everythin' in their path."

"Kill?" I asked. "All I want is for them to scare everyone. Show the people of this town that they can't mess with me and my family anymore."

"You need to get down there and stop 'em before they start killin' and eatin' those people."

If Mr. Mitchell said anything else, I didn't hear him. I ran out of his house and down the hill overlooking the town. Before I reached Main Street, I could already hear the screaming.

Pausing for a second, I swallowed hard and took a deep breath, then ran to Main Street. Since the zombies had left with my instructions, they had more than doubled in count. There were dozens of them attacking and tearing people limb from limb.

In front of the post office, there was a mother carrying her young child, shielding the baby from the zombie on her back. I ran to help.

"Take him please," she begged and threw the baby into my arms.

The baby was screaming for his mother, but she was already on the ground, her neck torn open. Blood sprayed my face. It was warm and tasted of copper.

"Stop!" I yelled at the zombie as he continued to tear at her neck and devour the flesh.

He looked up at me, but then his gaze shifted to the child in my arms. He rose to his feet and reached for the baby.

I backed away. "No, you leave him alone," I demanded.

The zombie turned and headed across the street to a married couple running to get in their car. The zombie grabbed the man and bit into his arm.

I couldn't watch anymore. Everywhere I turned, there was blood and body parts. Zombies moved from one person to the next, killing until they spotted a new victim.

Sheriff Wells came running down the street with a shotgun. He started aiming at random zombies, then fired. He hit them in the legs, arms, or chest.

They would fall down briefly but then would get back to their feet and continue their destruction. Finally, he hit one in the face and the zombie stayed down for good.

While looking for his next target, he made eye contact with me. "You did this. I know you did. You and your horrible sister." He aimed the shotgun at me and walked closer. "If I kill you, then this will all stop." He pumped the shotgun and an empty shell dropped to the ground.

Even with all the other noises around me, I only heard the hollow sound of that depleted shell hitting the ground. I knew he was going to kill me and there was nothing I could do to stop him.

Since I was still holding the baby, I turned my back to the sheriff in the hope I'd be able to shield the child from my fate.

A shot was fired and it rang in my ears. The baby screamed and I dropped him to the ground.

There was a burning pain in my shoulder, and everything moved in slow motion. I reached for my shoulder and looked at my hand. It was covered in blood.

I turned around to see the sheriff lying on the ground with a zombie tearing through his chest and ripping the organs from his body.

I was saved by the very creatures I'd created.

Looking down the street, the amount of carnage going on was unbelievable. Even more zombies had shown up, there had to be fifty or more now.

"Stop!" I screamed, but everything continued. "Stop!" I yelled again. Dropping to my knees, I began to cry. All I could do was watch everything play out in front of me. A small stream of blood trickled down the gutter in the street.

When I turned to look at the small child, an older man had picked him up.

"Where are you taking him?" I asked.

"This is my grandson. And now he'll never get to know his mother," the man said. He ran to a nearby car, put him in the backseat, and drove away.

I watched the carnage around me. Was this who I wanted to be? Was I the type of person who could live with herself after doing this to all these people?

I was torn up inside. I felt powerful, like no one could hurt me, but in order to feel that way I had to become a monster.

The zombies were finishing their rampage and coming to me for guidance; wanting to know what they should do next. As I looked at the group forming in front of me, I saw they were all covered in fresh blood.

Some of them were missing limbs, or the flesh was torn from their decomposing bodies. They'd taken a beating, but in the end accomplished exactly what I'd sent them out to do.

It was time to send them home—send them back to their final resting place.

I wasn't sure where they had all come from, so I said, "Return home."

One by one, they turned and walked away, disappearing around buildings and homes. After the last zombie was gone, I was left with only death.

Random body parts were strewn everywhere, the stream of blood had stopped flowing and now looked like red paint was drying in the gutter.

I would never do this again.

"Sydney? Are you listening to me?"

"Huh?"

"I just told you about my day and you sat there looking out the window. Have you even heard a single thing I've said?"

I looked around and realized I was back in the restaurant, sitting in the booth with my sister. "Sorry, I was thinking about the first time I raised zombies."

Sadie began to laugh. "It was so funny how they all started showing up at their homes. I could picture the looks on the faces of their families." She took a quick drink. "Why did you send them home?"

I could feel my face heat up. "I wasn't trying to send them to their homes, just back to wherever they came from."

She continued to laugh. "Don't be embarrassed because I'm laughing. I think it was funny. All the papers read: *The Dead Return!* Everyone was panicking."

"Well, I do have to agree with you on that one. The papers did play it up for a long time and that's why I can't call that many now."

"When I've done the killing, you've controlled the dead bodies very well. You've also learned how to stop a zombie before it loses control."

"But that was only one at a time," I said, pleading with her to change her mind about her plan.

"Fine, then I'll kill more next time for you to practice with," Sadie said with a smile on her face.

I shook my head and let it go. "Let's finish eating and we can talk more about this tonight."

She agreed and we finished lunch, but I knew this conversation was far from over and ultimately I would do what Sadie wanted.

I always did.

MANDIE'S ZOMBIES

DANA BELL

"Mandie? Why are all your dolls in there?" I stared at my five-year-old daughter in disbelief. Somehow, she'd managed to tie a bit of yarn around her toy box. The rest of her toys were scattered about on the dark brown carpet.

She looked so grown up with her 'I can't believe you asked me that' look on her round face. "Because they're zombies, Mom."

I groaned.

Zombies.

Zombies had invaded my house thanks to my teenage children who had grabbed onto the latest craze and watched hours and hours of the decaying monsters. Before that it had been vampires and werewolves and before that witches and dragons.

"Honey, there are no such things as zombies," I told her. I pulled my slowly graying black hair out of my face and reminded myself I need to keep it tied back. After all, my other daughter, Sandy, had given me a bunch of new scrunches for my birthday.

"Are too." She crossed her arms over her yellow t-shirt stained with peanut butter and grape jelly.

"No, there's not." My patience was running thin and I had to get to the store to buy a few things for dinner. "Please, untie your toy box and put your dolls back into their house." I pointed to the plastic pink structure in the corner.

"No." Instead of obeying me, she stacked a few stuffed animals on top of the box. "Now, they can't get out."

I heard the back door slam and my son yell, "Mom, what's to eat?" I swear that boy would be happy to eat everything in sight, twenty-four hours a day.

"There are some corn chips and salsa on the counter," I called back. I'd prepared his snack a few minutes ago.

"No meat?"

"I haven't gone to the store yet." I tapped my foot and stared at my youngest. She put another teddy bear on top and grinned at me. "Put your shoes on. We need to go to the store."

"Okay." She skipped across the room and retrieved her shoes from beneath a huge furry rabbit her grandmother had given her last Christmas.

Taking her hand, we left her messy bedroom and went into the kitchen. Carl and his friends were making short work on the snack I'd left and drinking down a ton of soda. They'd left the refrigerator door open and I closed it.

"Where's your sister?" I grabbed my bulging purse off the table and retrieved my sweater from the back of the dining room chair.

Carl shrugged. "Sandy's with her friends. They're doing a zombie crawl around the school." The boys shared a laugh. Their faces seemed a bit pale. "She should be home for dinner though." He leered at Mandie, who ducked behind my legs, her hands clinging to my jeans.

"Good." I grabbed my car keys off the peg by the back door. "I should be back in about an hour. Mandie's coming with me."

The boys laughed again and migrated toward the family room. I heard zapping sounds seconds later. They were playing one of those video games. Given their current fascination, I'm sure zombies were dying. I again took Mandie's hand and opened the back door.

"They're zombies," she said. "They wanted to eat me."

"Nonsense."

Warm sunshine bathed by face as I secured Mandie in her car seat. She was a bit small for her age and the law demanded I keep her in what she considered 'the baby chair' until she put on more weight.

She tugged at the belt. "Yuck."

"I know, honey." I slid the silver van door shut and got in. It started up, rumbling its way down the street and the few blocks to the grocery store. When we arrived, I went inside to purchase a roast, some potatoes and makings for a salad, the latter of which Carl wouldn't eat. Sandy however, wouldn't eat anything else.

"I want ice cream!" Mandie tried to reach the handle to a door in the frozen food aisle.

"No ice cream" I steered the shopping cart closer to the center. The harsh overhead lights glared down and I blinked. "What should I get for dessert?"

"Ice cream!" Mandie insisted, clapping her hands. Her dark hair hung down over her blue eyes. I really should have brushed it before we left. Maybe put in some of those pretty bows she liked.

Shaking my head, I selected instead some frozen strawberry fruit bars. They were still a sweet cold treat but without all the fat.

Mandie made a face and tried to crawl out of the cart. "Want out!"

"Stay put!" A glance at my watch told me how late I was running. Herb, my husband, would be home for work in about two hours. I wanted dinner on the table when he got home.

"Want out!" my daughter repeated, kicking her legs to emphasize her point.

"You stay there or else I'll hook these." I showed her the blue straps each cart had. She made a face but didn't try to get out again.

Quickly, I finished my shopping. I added some green beans and selected a bag of potatoes I'd now have to mash so they'd be ready on time, a huge pre-cooked roast from the deli and of course, a bag of lettuce and a few other vegetables for the salad.

"Can I have milk?" Mandie smiled at me sweetly.

I'd almost forgotten. I went back to the dairy aisle and grabbed a gallon of whole milk. Carl still refused to use a glass and I don't know how many times I'd caught him drinking out of the container. Sandy thought it was gross and refused to drink any. I kept reminding her women needed more calcium than men. She made a face and ignored me. Mandie didn't seem to care so I made sure she always had a glass when she asked.

"Chocolate?" Her blue eyes pleaded with me.

"Not today, dear." I hurried through the checkout and back out to the van. I secured Mandie in her car seat and loaded my grocery bags into the back. I slammed the rear door and pushed the cart back into the round up. As I opened the driver's door to get into my van, I noticed a man watching us intently. Was he drooling? I shook my head and started the engine.

"He's a zombie," Mandie said.

I'd heard enough about zombies. It was time to put an end to Carl and Sandy's craze. I decided to talk to them about it when I returned home.

On the drive back, I noticed the streets were oddly quiet. Usually, rush hour traffic was in full swing and children would be playing in front yards or on the sidewalk. I don't know how often I had to stomp on my brakes to keep from hitting one of them or some runaway ball.

"The zombies have come." Mandie started to sing one of her favorite songs.

I tried not to growl. Mandie was much too young to know about such disgusting creatures. Carl and Sandy needed to find a more harmless fascination.

As I pulled into the driveway, I saw that my husband's flashy red car was already there. Great. Now he'd grumble about dinner not being ready, as he sat in his throne before the huge flat screen TV hanging on the family room wall. That is, if he'd managed to wrest it away from game addicted teenagers.

I quickly unloaded the van, got Mandie out of her car seat, and opened the back door leading into the kitchen.

"What the…" I stared in horror at what had been my nice clean kitchen. Every cupboard had been opened and almost every box of food had been torn open. "Carl!"

My son shuffled in.

"What happened in here?" I demanded as I put down the grocery bags. Mandie skipped around me and I heard her bedroom door slam closed.

Carl shrugged. "We were hungry."

"Clean up this mess, now!" I couldn't start dinner until they did.

My son glared at me with red-tinged eyes. Was it my imagination or was his face a bit more ashen? Even his clothes seemed to hang on him while just this morning I was thinking I would have to go shopping for new ones because he seemed to have outgrown them—again.

"Clean this mess up now or else you'll get no dinner." I tapped my foot, my hands resting my hips.

"I'll report you to the school," he threatened.

"That hasn't been a threat since you were in grade school," I answered. Carl seemed to think the school was God or something. It was nonsense of course. I was his mother and I had the final say.

"Get busy. And if your friends are still here, they can help you." I marched off to greet my husband.

Herb was where I knew he'd be, watching TV, or his version of it. In his hand rested the remote and he was flipping through the channels. His suit, which I'd steamed this morning, was wrinkled and smelled of musty sweat.

"Hi, sweetie," I greeted as I bent over to kiss him.

"Hi," he grunted back, kissing me out of habit while his brown eyes kept track of the changing images.

"Dinner will be a bit late," I apologized.

He started to reply when a piercing scream and a small body charged into the family room. "They're gone!" Mandie screamed.

"What's gone?" After the day I'd had, I couldn't stand any more drama.

"My dolls!" Huge tears dripped down her cheeks.

Laughter drifted from the kitchen. Great. Carl and his friends must have done something with them.

My husband patted his lap. "Come here, Mandie." She curled up with him like it was the safest place to be. It both pleased and irked me.

I went into the kitchen to demand an explanation from my son. "What were you doing in your sister's bedroom?" Each of my children had been taught to respect the privacy of their siblings. They didn't always. I knew that. There would be a punishment.

"I heard a noise." Carl tossed an empty box into the trash. It thunked as it went into the plastic container.

His friends were gone. Typical teenagers. Make a mess and leave someone behind to get the blame and clean up.

"You couldn't ask your father to investigate?" I glared at my son.

"He wasn't here." Carl scratched what looked like a small bite on his arm. I'd probably have to call the pest control man again.

Spiders seemed to like our house. They invade on a regular basis and I was always swatting them with a newspaper. Their bloody insides left dark smudges on my nice white walls.

"Was Sandy here when this happened?" I pointed at the mess.

"Nah." Carl closed a couple of cupboards. I frowned. Was that a bit of white fur I saw sticking out of one? "She went to the movies with some of her girlfriends."

She went without asking—again. Sandy had done that several times during the past year. She seemed to think fifteen was old enough to make her own decisions. Her father and I had explained many times how it wasn't, but she kept testing us.

The way Carl was slowly moving, I knew my kitchen wouldn't get cleaned up if I didn't help. With a sigh because I really didn't want to, I pitched in, got dinner started, and sent my son to his room after unplugging his computer from the internet so he couldn't play games or chat with his friends for hours at a time. He rolled his eyes and glared at me. I didn't care. It was a fair punishment.

I have no idea what time dinner actually was ready, and we finally ate, Herb, Mandie and I. The rest of the evening was routine with giving Mandie a bath, cleaning up the kitchen again, and saying goodnight to my husband who wouldn't come to bed until after the news was over. I checked on Carl. He was asleep, slumped over his desk, his Math homework spread all over the maple-colored wood. Sandy still hadn't come home but Herb promised to deal with her when she did.

Laying in bed, and staring at the ceiling, I reflected what a horrible day it had been. All that zombie talk from Mandie; I really did need to change Carl and Sandy's viewing habits. It was infecting their younger sister.

As I drifted off, I felt a pinch on my arm. It itched. I really would have to call the exterminator in the morning. The spiders were out of control. I swatted at it and my hand encountered something fuzzy.

Startled, I turned on the lamp on my nightstand and looked down. Staring up at me was a small, blonde-haired doll with blood dripping from its mouth. Its fashionable clothes were torn and its skin was an ugly gray.

"What the hell?" I sat up and found myself looking into my husband's ashen face. I hadn't heard him come into our bedroom.

"You'll be one of us, now," he said.

"What?" My eyes drifted to my two teen children who stood beside him. At least Sandy was finally home. Though I narrowed my blue eyes, she also seemed too pale and her clothes, which I normally objected to because they showed more skin than any teen age girl should, also hung loosely on her lean body.

"Mandie was right," Carl said, a smile touching his peeling lips. "The dolls are zombies." He laughed harshly. "Or perhaps I should say, 'zombie makers.' "

"They bit all of us," Sandy added and rubbed her hands together. Flakes fell to the carpet. I would have to vacuum them up in the morning, I thought. "We made sure all our friends got nibbled on, too."

"I was bitten while watching TV," Herb said. He pointed to his finger. His clothes smelled even worse now, like a decaying fish.

"Mandie." I was terrified for my youngest. Had she also fallen to the insanity now engulfing my family?

"Not to worry." Herb rubbed his stomach. "We left you some dinner downstairs."

They all laughed in a manner that caused my slowly-chilling blood to feel even colder. "What have you done?" I pushed the covers back. My veins were turning a putrid purple and my skin was now white.

"Nothing you wouldn't agree with, dear." Herb stood back as another figure shuffled in. "Mandie, why don't you give your mother a hug."

My precious five-year-old came to me. Mandie's purple night gown dragged on the floor and her flesh was gray. Her normally pretty blue eyes were now puffy and red.

"Hi, Momma," she said with a wicked grin. "I told you the dolls were zombies."

STRANGE DAY

J. L. PETTY

"**M**an, I hate traffic." I leaned over and turned the radio down. Annoyed, I waited like the hundreds of other taxis till the jam opened up. At least the meter was running.

"If you don't mind me asking, what is it exactly you do for a living, exactly?" I stared out the window at the pedestrians on the busy sidewalk in Times Square, then looked down at my digital watch. It read 10:32 p.m. The people in the street looked like colorful pieces of construction paper on a black background. I leaned my head back on my headrest and listened to the rain splatter against the window. My stomach screamed for French fries. *I'd kill for some McDonald's right now*, I thought.

"I'm an actor," the man sitting in my backseat mumbled.

"Oh wow, I have a big shot in my cab. I can't wait to tell the wife at home, what movies have I seen you in?"

The man, wearing a Yankees baseball cap, stopped doing his crossword puzzle. He looked over the magazine and said, "I've been in a few movies; did you see that movie *Fight Club*?"

I turned and smiled at him. "Hey, that sounds familiar… It'll come to me. But I know I've seen you somewhere else. I don't get to the movies much. I'm always in this cab." I squirmed in my seat.

"How long have you been a taxi driver?" He took off his baseball cap and placed it next to him.

"I've been driving a cab for about a year, give or take. I got laid off from the post office, which I hated anyway so it wasn't that big of a loss." I scratched my nose. "I collected unemployment till it ran out, and then I really needed the money. Wish I could get paid gazillions of dollars to be in a movie. What's that luxury feel like?"

In a hoarse voice, he offered me a bit of advice. "You know, the grass is never greener. I'd trade places with you in a heartbeat, just to spend more time with my family and have my privacy back. The paparazzi are relentless."

"Listen, pal, I'm a fifty year old taxi driver with a too high mortgage and bad blood pressure. I bet beautiful models probably throw themselves at you all the time and everyone wants to take a picture with you. You're a big shot, be grateful." The quiet drizzle against the window was now a fat splash. I stared at the dried-up mustard stain on my shirt that hadn't gone away. I attempted to wipe the stain without success for the third time that night. Traffic wasn't getting any better either. "Damn it." Realizing I was cursing out loud, I turned to the man. "I'm sorry, traffic is slow today."

"It's fine. I'm not in a hurry. You know, I'm kind of glad you don't recognize me. It's rare for me." The man kept clicking his pen over and over again. "Speaking of pictures, when a paparazzo snaps a photo of me, it feels disgusting. You feel like you're under a microscope. If I'm going to the gym so I'm not dressed up, I have to make sure they don't get a picture, because it would be all over the magazines tomorrow about how awful I looked that day. I never get a break."

"You big shots are always complaining. I'd do it for the women." I leaned further down in my cracked-leather seat to get comfortable. "The women would be the best part about Hollywood."

"You'd think, but fame isn't all it's cracked up to be. Actually, the women are the worse part. Short skirts in the middle of winter, stalking you everywhere you go, ripping your clothes—it's awful. Those women will do almost anything to get a piece of me. It pisses my wife off a lot and it's hard to stop them." He reached into his pocket and pulled out his phone. "They're always flashing me, even in front of my children, and I hate it as a parent. You'd think they'd respect my children at least."

While listening to his ramblings, traffic started to pick up. "Yeah, that does sound kinda rough. Looks like the jam is breaking up. I should have you at your hotel in about ten minutes."

"Thanks." He adjusted himself in his seat and put his baseball cap back on, then he reached into the front pocket of his jacket, took out a pair of eye glasses, and put them on.

"Is that your disguise?" I glanced at the rearview mirror.

"Sort of, I guess." He turned to unbuckle his seat belt.

"Well, I'd rather be a big shot actor any day. Being a taxi driver sucks, and it's dangerous. I should get paid a lot more than tips and an hourly wage. I was robbed last month at gunpoint, by some punk teenager. The worst part about it was I didn't get a good glimpse of the kid. So when the cops asked, I couldn't tell 'em nothing accept that the jerk was wearing a Lakers jersey. There are millions of whack jobs in New York, and it seems like most of them end up in my back seat."

"That's awful, I'm glad you made it out alive." The actor took out his wallet from his back jean pocket.

"Yeah, me too." I glanced at the meter. It read $52.50.

We were approaching the Hilton hotel. I made a sharp turn into the next lane to pull into the driveway, and of course I didn't signal. Suddenly, I felt a sharp jolt from behind my cab and could hear metal ripping from my bumper. In a matter of seconds, the cab dipped and tilted sideways. When I came to a stop I glanced into the backseat, on the edge of panic. "Are you okay, buddy?"

"Yes, I'm fine." The actor was touching himself to feel if he was okay. "Look, I have an appointment and I didn't see anything so I just need to pay and get going. How much do I owe you?"

The meter said $55.80 now and I told him.

"Here, keep the change." Then he was gone, the three twenties he'd tossed me lying on the seat next to me.

The man already forgotten, I opened my cab door and climbed out. The night air felt cool against my face. Like a detective, I circled my taxi. I could see an enormous dent embedded in my rear bumper. *It was the last thing I needed.*

"What's the matter with you? Didn't you see me, you idiot!" I hit the hood of the brown, rusted Volkswagen that had hit my cab.

"Hey screw you, pal." The driver of the Volkswagen stuck his arm out of his window and raised his fist in anger at me. "You didn't signal. I'm not a damn mind reader. You damn cabbies. You think you own the streets of New York!"

Before I could even think to say another word to the idiot in the Volkswagen, my thoughts were interrupted by a dozen men and women charging at my cab from across the street.

What the hell? Is this some kind of joke? Is this some kind of publicity stunt?

Unaware, the actor that had left my cab was walking up the driveway for the Hilton. He was suddenly grabbed by an enormous sea of what sure looked a hell of a lot like honest-to-goodness zombies.

They swarmed him like a pack of bees on a bucket of honey and the actor screamed loudly as the zombies tackled him like a football team.

I stood on the sidewalk bewildered. My feet felt glued to the pavement as I watched them rip his limbs apart. It was then that I realized this wasn't a joke, it was *real*.

There were hundreds of men, women, and children with decayed arms and rotten yellow teeth. Their clothes were tattered and they moaned uncontrollably. Their flesh was peeling and their eyes were bright red like a stop light. As they bit into the actor's flesh, dark blood stained their mouths. It was disgusting.

My eyes were big as saucers… *I got to get the hell outta here!* I thought.

I spun around quicker than a toy top. The fear I felt shot adrenaline through my body as I ran through the streets of New York. I could feel them chasing me

They're gaining on me!

I felt myself panting and getting tired. *I have to keep going…* Thoughts ran through my mind like newsreels. *Where am I gonna go? Where am I gonna hide? Is this the end of the world? Some kind of plague?*

A church! My heart jumped for joy when I saw a Catholic church come into view as I rounded a corner. *Those evil things…they won't come in here.* Panting, I dashed onto the property and opened the large doors at the top of the stone steps, slamming them closed after I was inside. Tears of fear rolled down my cheeks as I tried to slow my breathing. I tried to rationalize what I'd seen, but no matter how much I tried, it still remained the same. My hands were shaking. *At least I'm safe…*

I walked deeper into the church. It was empty, the tall ceiling covered in cobwebs. It was dark like a cave. From the front where the podium was, where the priest would give his sermon each Sunday, I saw a dark and shadowy figure pop up from behind the podium. Before I could move, the figure began charging towards me.

Is that Father Thomas? I wondered as the figure coalesced into a man, who was wearing the dark vestments of a priest.

Our bodies collided a second later. I fell backwards like a tortoise onto its back, the man on top of me. One of Father Thomas' eyes was hanging from its socket like a Christmas tree ornament. He bit into the side of my neck like a vampire and I screamed for help and in pain.

I struggled to push him off me, but his strength seemed super human and was too much to overcome. I began to grow faint from blood loss and I looked down to see the good Father gnawing on my arm, like it was a piece of beef jerky. I felt myself getting dizzy…and I couldn't fight anymore.

Then everything went black.

Where am I? I was awakened by sprinkles of ice cold water on my face.

"Lord, wash away this man's pain and cleanse his body." The Voodoo practitioner flicked water and herbs all over my chewed-up body. *Who is this woman? Why am I back in my apartment?*

She was a slim woman in her late fifties or early sixties, with long dreadlocks, her skin as dark as a moonless night. She had a heavy Louisianan accent.

"Lord, let the spirits cleanse him, cleanse him from this sickness." She continued to sprinkle the herb water on my mangled face. I was lying in bed, and half dead, chunks of flesh missing from my arms and legs.

I hope this works, I prayed.

"Sam! You're awake. I thought the zombies killed you." Cynthia, my wife, squeezed my hand tight. Her face lit up and she grinned from ear to ear.

"Where's my cab?" I mumbled. "Why aren't I in a hospital?"

"This woman found you. You were bleeding to death. You were attacked by a zombie. She got your address from your driver's license in your wallet and called me. I drove right over to get you and with her help, we managed to get you home." Cynthia's smile faded. "Those monsters are all over the place. I swear it's the end of the world. We couldn't take you to a hospital because it's not safe. The hospitals are overloaded already. Sam? Sam, are you okay?"

"Yes... please stop the pain... please stop the bleeding." I mumbled.

"Child, he's losin' too much blood. I'm not sure if I can save him." She placed the bowl of water and herbs on the nightstand. She had given up on me. She started to put on her black trenchcoat and proceeded to walk towards the bedroom door. "I'm sorry, child, it's too late for your man, he's a goner."

She's my last hope. Cynthia don't let her leave, please!

"Please, I'll pay anything. Money is no object," Cynthia called out. "I just want my Sam to get better. I'll pay anything." Cynthia rushed to her purse on the nightstand. She searched for her check book like a kid looking for candy in a Halloween bucket. "How much money do you want? Name your price." She pulled out her wallet.

"Ten thousand dollars." The woman folded her arms stiffly. "There are still no guarantees, but if you pay me, I will do what I can."

Cynthia froze like a statue in a museum. "That's a lot of money, I don't know." She closed her check book.

Agitated, I moaned.

"You want to save his life don't you, child? You shouldn't put a price on your man's life." She stared at Cynthia accusingly and then at me.

I coughed. My skin was pale and I had dark circles under my eyes, as if I hadn't slept in years.

Pay her! I don't want to die. My eyes went wide as I tried to convey my thoughts. I couldn't speak, only gasp.

Beads of sweat streamed down Cynthia's face. "Why is it so much money?"

"You shouldn't ask questions, child. I'm practically bringing your husband back from the dead. He only has a short time left and I don't have time for your foolishness." She turned around and walked towards the door. "I'm leaving."

"No, wait!" Cynthia reached out her hand like a baby wanting a pacifier. She picked up the check book and started writing the check. "Who do I make this out to?"

"Leave it blank, I'll fill it in later, just sign it." She took her coat off and snatched the check from my wife's hands.

"Are you sure you know what you're doing?" Cynthia asked.

I gazed up at the Voodoo priestess for reassurance.

"Black magic can save or doom anyone, child. You just have to believe. Do you believe?" She glanced down at me on the bed.

"Yes, yes." Cynthia nodded. "Just save him, I'll do anything you say."

"Fine, I will hold you to that promise, child. Now, I need three white candles, chalk, garlic, and fresh blood." She barked the orders at Cynthia, who obeyed and went off to search through the house for the items.

Cynthia, please hurry!

"I have everything except the blood." Cynthia knelt down and poured the supplies on the floor at the old woman's feet. "How is he doing?" She picked up the candles and started to light them.

"Not good. We have to begin. He is close to death." The Voodoo priestess grabbed the chalk and drew a circle on the hardwood floor. She grabbed two pieces of garlic and placed them on my hairy chest, ignoring the blood already there.

"We will have to use your blood." She pulled out a pocket knife. "Give me your hand, child." She reached out for Cynthia, who hesitated, then begrudgingly gave her hand to the old woman. She cut the tip of Cynthia's finger and blood immediately welled up. Cynthia frowned. The old woman held Cynthia's finger over my lips and let some of my wife's blood drip into my mouth.

I resisted at first, but I was too weak to close my mouth.

"Autume sady ish moth fron. Autume sady ish moth fron." The old woman chanted as warm blood slid into my mouth.

All of a sudden, I began to tremble. My hand flailed out and hit the lamp on my nightstand. It crashed to the floor and shattered into a hundred pieces. And then I felt myself getting stronger.

What's happening to me?

"Please stop!" Cynthia snatched her hand away and fell backwards onto the floor. She struggled to get up.

The bedroom was spinning faster than a roller coaster ride as my eyes rolled up into the back of my head. I could barely speak but slowly I began to form words. "What…did…you do…to me?" I whispered.

"I saved your life." The old woman started putting on her coat, a satisfied smile on her wrinkled lips. "I sacrificed your wife to save you." She stuffed the check in her pocket.

"You have five minutes to live, child." She looked at Cynthia coldly.

Cynthia looked like death, her skin already becoming pale.

She'd tricked us!

"When you make a deal with the Devil, be prepared to pay him in full," she chuckled to herself as she closed the bedroom door behind her.

"Cynthia?" I sat up slowly. With renewed strength, I crawled out of bed. I felt stronger than ever, despite my wounds and loss of blood.

"Cynthia, are you all right?" I stumbled towards my wife, who still lay on the floor. "What's happening to you? Honey, speak to me?" I held her close to me. "Cynthia, what's wrong?"

Her breaths grew shorter and shorter. Her eyes turned to me and I saw the life leave them, and with one last gasp, she quietly died in my arms.

Grief filled me as I held her still form. Tears weld up in my eyes and stung as they remained unshed.

I was so sad, but there was another feeling as well, something more primal. I was *hungry*. I couldn't control myself as I sank my teeth into her neck. My grief began to fade. As difficult as it was, I continued to eat away at my wife.

Oh God, I'm so ashamed.

The zombie in me quickly took over as I thirsted for her blood, her flesh.

What have I done?

My mouth was stained with dark blood and gore hung from my chin. I could feel myself rotting from the inside out and a fire burned within me, a fire that could only be quenched with the flesh of my wife.

I felt so guilty at what I was doing but at the same time, it felt oh so good.

I'm still so hungry… Cynthia… I'm sorry.

Looking back, I had to admit, it was a very strange day.

FINISHING LAST

ALYN DAY

The metal bolts holding the rusted-out fire escape to the crumbling brick building overlooking the alleyway between Mr. Yan's House of Wok and Sunny Side Pets, began to groan and whine in protest almost before Julie had fully begun her ascent.

A flash of panic streaked through her nervous system like a bolt of lightning, leaving a bright burning afterglow in its wake.

A mantra repeated in pitiful desperation, *I'm going to die*, sing-songed in her head, echoing in the madness like a nursery rhyme.

The dead things stalked into the alley below her, stumbling and shuffling and knocking each other out of the way in their desire to lay hands on her living flesh. She pulled herself up higher on the rotting metal ladder, despite the knowledge that it probably would not support her weight. There was simply no other option left to her. She clutched her daughter to her chest and stared up at the bright blue sky, blinking back tears of sadness and desperation, as she prayed to a god she no longer felt connected to as some sort of savior. If not for herself, then at least for her innocent little daughter.

The stench was overwhelming, a mixture of spoiled meat, rancid milk, rot, mold, death and decay. The hollow moans of the undead filled the air, harkening the end of Julie and all she held dear. She tentatively pulled herself up another rung, hands shaking so badly she feared she might lose her grip entirely. The bolts near the top segment had begun to pull away from the wall. Ancient brick dust, like some sort of *coup poudre*, drifted down onto the clamoring horde beneath her feet. Julie squeezed her eyes closed, a hushed whisper on her lips as the metal creaked and groaned in protest of the burden she had forced upon it. The bolts pulled free of the wall just a bit further and the ancient ironwork slid that much closer to the grasping, fetid hands waiting mere feet below.

Julie couldn't scream, she could barely even cry as the hand of death raked its icy fingers down her spine. She tried not to look at the alley below, mindful of the advice she had heard in one form or another from a young age, but it was impossible to resist. Hideous things looked up at her; mirthless grinning mouths stretched by rigor; dried up, decaying skin, bony fingers, sunken eyes and oozing, festering wounds. They no longer resembled the human beings they once were; they had become lost entirely to the infection that had claimed nearly all of the Earth's population.

One of the metal anchors near the top of the fire escape gave way completely and the ladder canted to the right, swinging out from the wall by nearly a foot as it slid towards the monsters in the alley. There were only half a dozen of them or so, by Julie's panicked count, but it was more than enough to spell certain death for her and her nearly four-year-old daughter, Celia.

They had made it this far, survived the infection and the ensuing collapse of society, made it out of the city by themselves , and it was all going to end here, in a trash-filled alley somewhere outside of Nashua, New Hampshire.

The ladder slid once more and Julie screamed involuntarily. Only a few more inches and the taller of those things would be able to reach the bottom rung and pull her down into the clamoring hands and cavernous mouths of the waiting, hungry dead.

When the shots rang out, Julie's confused mind couldn't immediately make sense of them. Her brain, consumed by a heady mixture of adrenaline and fear, spun and swam with confusion.

She had initially believed they were the sounds of the remaining bolts giving up the ghost and sending her and Celia plunging to their doom, but the ladder hadn't moved.

Her frantic gaze fell again on the ravenous creatures below. To her surprise, three of them lay on the ground, silent and still, one missing everything above its fetid throat. As she watched, another thunderous roar rang out and another of the walking dead fell, a hole through its forehead.

Julie's wide eyes searched the perimeter, scanning the windows, the buildings, the rooftops, until at last she spied her savior.

A man with close cropped brown hair wearing a dark turtleneck under a black Kevlar vest was kneeling on the roof above the crumbling brick and faltering ladder. He dispatched the remaining zombies with two more well-placed shots—from what looked to the untrained Julie like some sort of a rifle—before slinging his gun over his shoulder and gathering a length of rope. He leaned down over the edge of the roof, and extended the lifesaving rope to Julie's desperately clutching hands. She missed it twice, but on the third time managed to hang on as the stranger in black pulled her and her daughter up onto the roof.

No sooner had she set foot on firm ground than Julie's eyes teared up and she began to tremble. She threw her arms around the man, who appeared somewhat off-put by her gesture, and sobbed her gratitude. "Thank you! Oh, God, thank you! You saved us!" she gasped. "You saved me and my baby girl!"

The man in the dark clothing gently untangled himself from her grasp, stepping backwards and looking embarrassed. "It was really nothing, ma'am." He looked at his shoes and fidgeted like a schoolboy unprepared to speak in front of the class. He wore dark cargo-style pants and heavy black combat boots. Near where he'd been positioned on the roof, was a large black nylon backpack.

Julie could see the butt of a shotgun sticking out of the largest pocket.

Julie put Celia down and began looking her over for bites or scratches. The man at last looked up. His eyes were piercingly blue. "Can I ask what you were doing out here?" he asked, trying his best to sound authoritative and commanding but really just came across as inquisitive and polite.

Julie looked up from her daughter's round little face. More tears were on the verge of spilling out. "She was…she was hungry…" Julie stammered. "We were just going to find some food when those…those *things* came out of nowhere. They surrounded us. It happened so quickly and…and…" Her breath hitched in her throat. "If you hadn't come along when you did, I don't… I don't think we'd be alive right now." She broke down into tears again.

The man went over and dug through his backpack, pulling out a packet of beef jerky and some cookies in a zip lock baggy. He knelt down and offered them to the small girl, smiling. She gingerly took them from him after looking back at her mother to see if it was okay. Julie nodded emphatically, wiping away her tears with the backs of her hands.

"My name's John," he said, looking at Julie over Celia's small shoulder, as she wolfed down the cookies and jerky. "What's yours?"

"Julie," she replied, extending a now-steady hand past her daughter. "My daughter is Celia."

"It's nice to meet both of you," John said, for once dropping the false bravado. "Are you guys with some sort of a group or…" He trailed off as Julie's facade once again began to crumble. "We were with… my husband… he…" She pulled herself together after a moment. "I mean, no. It's just us."

John nodded thoughtfully. "Well, two girls out by themselves ought to have some sort of protection…" He reached into his bag and pulled out a small pistol. "Do you know how to use one of these?"

Julie shook her head.

"Well," he said, looking around, "I guess you could stick with me. I mean, my group's got a base set up about five miles from here. I'm out on a scouting mission until tomorrow, but you can stay with me till then and we'll all go back together. You'll have to pull your weight, of course, but there's safety in numbers and I…I just wouldn't feel right about leaving you two out here all alone."

Julie threw her arms around him once more. "I don't know how to thank you!" she said, voice trembling. "Ever since this nightmare began people have been so…so cruel. Almost worse than those monsters! You've been so kind to us. Thank you! Just thank you!"

"It's nothing, ma'am. Really. Nothing at all. I reckon we could use a cook or something anyway. You're doing us a favor. Really." Once again, John disentangled himself from the emotional mother. He picked up his backpack and slung it over his shoulder, opposite the rifle.

"Well, if you're sticking with me, you'd best come along now. We need to make camp before it gets dark." He marched across the roof and pulled open a door that had been prevented from closing all the way with a cinderblock. He kicked the cinderblock to the side and held the door open for Julie and Celia.

At the foot of the stairs, he gestured at the pair to be quiet. Opening the door slowly, he searched the area quickly and quietly for any stray zombies that might have wandered in. Finding no threat, he invited the girls into the lobby before leading them out into the deserted city streets beyond.

They spent that night in an abandoned liquor store. The building was small and run down, but easily defensible due to the pre-existing bars over the few small windows, and the slide-down metal gate over the front door. It was the lone remaining entry point, as the rear door was pinned closed by a delivery truck. Julie volunteered to take watch, but John insisted he wasn't tired.

She slid from consciousness due to sheer exhaustion in seconds, the shadow of a smile playing across her lips as John laid a jacket over her sleeping daughter beside her.

Morning brought new challenges, as in the light of day, the group could no longer cling to the shadows.

"All right," John said, polishing off the rest of his piss-warm energy drink. "This isn't gonna be easy. I've made this trip myself before, but never with a…a…child in tow. We'll have to travel overland, by foot. That means being quick, being quiet, and most of all, staying alert." He knelt down and looked Celia in the eyes. "Can you do that, honey? Can you keep on the lookout for those things? And let your mommy know if you see one?"

Celia nodded, smiling, and John stood up, ruffling her hair playfully. Julie was amazed by how comfortable she felt around this man in the dark clothing. She supposed it had something to do with him rescuing her and Celia from certain death the day before, but perhaps it was more than that. He seemed kind, and kindness was in short supply in this new world.

After scarfing down a quick meal of granola bars and canned peaches, John put Julie to work scavenging for anything useful remaining in the liquor store. Under the counter, she found a handful of shotgun shells—but no shotgun—some aspirin, and a few tattered nudie mags. The latter she shoved further into their hiding space, blushing with embarrassment. Other than that meager haul, there was little left in the store, save for broken glass and sticky puddles of dried-up alcohol. John packed up his belongings and added the aspirin and shells to his inventory.

Without another word, the trio headed out.

The reality of the world outside the liquor store came crashing back on Julie as she stood just beyond the door, shielding her eyes with her hand, and blinking in the sunshine as she adjusted to the harsh light of day.

Cars were overturned and crashed into buildings and light poles, a few of them still smoldering. Bodies littered the sidewalk in various states of decay. Some appeared mostly whole, while others were missing limbs or even heads. Dried blood was smeared and spattered on everything and the smell was awful. Despite the amount of meat lying around for the taking, Julie could spot no carrion eaters. In fact, other than John and Celia, she spied no movement at all. Not even a breeze to rustle the hair of the cadavers.

John caught her attention and put his finger to his lips to indicate silence. He slung the rifle to his front, ready to fire at the first sign of trouble. He gently corralled Celia behind him with his free arm, and Julie brought up the rear.

The ragtag group made their way across the street and down an alley. Overturned garbage cans and disarrayed dumpsters blocked their path. Celia tripped as she tried to clamber over such an obstacle, causing a metal trash can to roll noisily for a few feet. John and Julie held their breaths, listening for any sign that the zombies had been alerted to their position. After a few moments of continued silence, they moved on.

They were just coming around the corner of another building, when without warning, Celia ran forward before Julie could stop her.

"Daddy!" she cried, her chubby little legs propelling her faster than Julie could follow. To her utter horror, her daughter raced straight at the lumbering form of a recently risen zombie. His eyes were cloudy and covered in a fine film of dust and grit. Zombies didn't blink, after all. His skin had taken on a waxy yellow pallor. His lips were coated in grime and gore, and one of his hands looked as if the flesh had been peeled from it; strings of gristle and rubbery sinew hung from glistening white bone. Despite the radical changes, there was no mistaking her husband. Julie fell to her knees, frozen.

John took aim and sent the zombie reeling with a shot to the chest, followed moments later by another to the head, shattering the skull and spraying the sidewalk with gooey bits of brain matter and shards of whitish bone. Celia broke into tears and began wailing; Julie remained all but useless in the wake of her husband's second passing.

After a moment, she looked up. John slowly lowered the gun and approached her, a look of deep sympathy playing over his strong features. "I'm…" He searched for words. "I'm so very sorry."

Julie nodded, then sniffled the last of her tears and wiped her runny nose with her sleeve. She gathered up her sobbing daughter and cradled Celia in her arms, trying to calm her. John did his best to look unaffected and put his effort into maintaining their perimeter.

After a few minutes during which Julie struggled to keep from looking at the desecrated corpse of the man she'd married, John put a solemn hand on Julie's trembling shoulder.

"Look, I am really and truly sorry for your loss." His voice faltered as he struggled for words. "But we need to keep moving. More of those things could show up at any moment."

Julie nodded and waited for him to lead the way.

John once more took the lead, Julie following close behind, while carrying her small daughter, who once in a while mewled a plaintive, lonely sob. Celia looked over Julie's shoulder in the direction from which they had come, the direction in which her father still lay, cold and alone and partially eaten by the things that had turned him into one of them.

The city streets stretched out before the trio like an asphalt version of The River Styx. Surrounded by death, perilous and treacherous, the path ahead would not be an easy one. Julie did her best to calm her distraught daughter, but after the incident with her husband, it was all but impossible.

Luckily, there didn't seem to be very many of the walking dead around. The few that the group did manage to come across were dispatched quickly and efficiently by John's skilled hands. Julie was lucky to have been found by the lone gunman, as she had come to think of him. She and Celia probably wouldn't have lasted the night on their own, even if they had survived the incident on the ladder in the alley.

Julie had never been much of a survivalist. She'd been raised in the city by an architect father and an English professor mother, and both had emphasized higher learning over more practical skills. Julie herself had gone to school for computer science and had specialized in programming. She'd landed a job with a fairly prestigious software development company before becoming pregnant with Celia and quitting her job to raise her child at her husband's insistence.

Mark had been a good man; patient and kind, loving and devoted. He's been an excellent father to Celia and a good provider. He was certainly no great outdoorsman himself, but years of experience as a boy scout, coupled with summers spent camping and hiking in the woods of upstate New York, had better prepared him to deal with the world as it was now—a post zombie plague.

Julie hadn't known what they would do without Mark to show her how to purify water and clean pigeon and squirrel carcasses so that they had fresh meat. When he was bitten, she'd tried to trick herself into believing that he would be all right, that he was somehow immune to the virus. When he'd eventually succumbed to the fever that swept through him like a brushfire, she had simply taken Celia and left the family's tiny shelter. Not really knowing what to do or where to go, she'd simply drifted aimlessly until finding herself trapped in an alley on a fire escape, and surrounded by bloodthirsty ghouls. She thanked whatever god could have allowed something like this to happen to her that John had come along to see her and Celia's predicament, and to then save them.

To the average suburbanite or city dweller, five miles seems like nothing. Hell, many of them traveled that far or further just for their morning coffee. But in a world without motorized transportation, and through a veritable minefield of dangers, including scavengers, feral animals, treacherous landscape, looters, and of course the walking dead, five miles seemed like fifty. Or maybe even five hundred.

It took the ragtag trio the better part of the morning, all told about four and a half hours, to traverse the distance. At the end of that span of time, they found themselves on the outskirts of the city, staring up at a large warehouse.

The windows had been reinforced with boards and heavy-looking sheets of metal. Signs, maybe, Julie thought, or some sort of siding. The building itself was a dusty brown. It was surrounded by a ten foot tall fence topped by an intimidating coil of razor wire. "Wow!" Julie whispered. "Did you do all of this yourself?"

John smiled shyly. "Well, no," he admitted. "Not all of it. The fence was already here when I found the place. All I did was board up the windows and secure the perimeter, that's all."

"Well, whatever you did, the two of us are grateful. You've been so kind. You're such a nice person." The words sounded silly even to Julie's ears.

John blushed and looked away. "We should get inside." He unlocked an enormous padlock holding a heavy chain together around a large chain-link gate, which had wheels on the bottom so it could be opened easily. He led the girls inside and re-secured the gate. He slipped the key back into his shirt before dashing ahead and opening the door for his newfound friends. Julie barely had time to register the emptiness of the building before her world exploded in bright red stars and she hit the floor, unconscious.

When she came to—maybe hours later, maybe minutes—she opened her eyes slowly. The back of her head throbbed painfully and her neck felt sticky. She looked around for her daughter and panicked when she didn't see her. But after another moment, she found her, locked inside a large, wire-mesh, dog cage. Her eyes were huge, scared and red from crying.

Julie was trying to make sense of her predicament when John strode up to her, smiling. His demeanor had completely changed.

"Mornin' sunshine!" he grinned.

"Wha…what happened?" she asked, confused.

John's face changed once more, this time becoming a mask of anger and agitation. He backhanded Julie savagely.

"I happened, bitch!" he snarled, then laughed. It was his laughter that Julie found most chilling. There was no sign of the shy, kind man who had saved her and her daughter, no sign of anything human at all. "Let's see how nice you think I am now!" he leered.

Julie's eye was already swelling shut from the impact, but she heard the sound of John's fly being unzipped and his pants being pulled down. It wasn't long before she began to wish that the zombies had gotten her after all.

SPREADING THE SPORE

SUZANNE ROBB

The spore had waited for millions of years. When it first arrived on Earth, nothing but large creatures with sharp teeth roamed the planet.

They were easy to possess and control, but not compatible partners; eventually they all died, unable to adapt to the changes within their bodies.

Then insects and other animals arrived. The spore could once again spread, but there was a problem.

The only remaining spore sample was buried deep beneath the surface of the Earth in the petrified carcass of one of the creatures with large teeth.

With no other choice but to wait, the spore hibernated, waiting for a time when it would be uncovered and could once again coat the world with its presence.

Thousand of years passed, and then the day finally came. After several earthquakes, and many polar ice cap shifts later, the spore laid mere feet below the surface.

A rather ambitious ant colony awakened it, and within seconds they were infected.

They worked quick and efficient, removing as much of the spore as possible, then placed it on tree branches for when taller beings would pass by.

Nothing touched it, and the birds and other animals seemed too smart and stayed away.

The spore waited, knowing eventually something would come along. Something that would help spread the spore, and destroy the world.

"See, Jake, I told you all we needed was a weekend away. You've been so tense lately," Gina said.

Jake Rogers glanced over at his girlfriend and held back the comment on the tip of his tongue. He had been tense, but the stupid camping trip had been the cause.

"Yeah, you were right, dear. But I hope my allergies don't act up, and we have to watch out for bears. Not to mention we don't have any cell reception if we get into trouble."

Gina slammed the car door, then lifted a cooler of food. Jake watched as she walked to the dilapidated picnic table each campsite provided. Why did he agree to this? He hated nature; it was full of dirty things, dangerous things, all sorts of things he didn't like.

"Jake, you really need to relax. You're an absolute stress ball. Just take a breath of this fresh air. When was the last time you didn't inhale something with exhaust fumes?"

"We have an air purifier in the apartment." Jake hoped what he said didn't come out as childish it sounded.

"Jake, I love you, but if you can't live without technology and just enjoy being with me for the weekend, I'm leaving."

Jake sighed. He loved Gina and knew she was right, but he would never tell her.

"Okay, we camp then," he said and joined her at the table.

She smiled at him.

"Great, let me set this place up. You go take a walk or something. I'll have everything ready by the time you get back." She gave him a quick kiss on the lips, then turned away with her hands on her hips and surveyed the campsite.

Jake made his exit, knowing that when Gina set her mind to something, there would be hell to pay if he got in her way. He grabbed the mosquito repellent and coated his body with a generous amount, then rolled his pant legs tight to ward off ticks, put on a hat to protect his hair from falling stuff, and made sure the bear mace was hanging from his belt.

With a forced smile, he headed out to commune with nature, or whatever people did when they took walks into the perils of the unknown. Jake was a city boy, born and bred. He'd never gone camping before, and his only experiences with foliage was at the local park and the flower shop he went to when he bought flowers for Gina.

A noise off to his left caused him to stop and reach for his mace. He forced himself to look in that direction, expecting to see a cougar, bear, or perhaps a lion. Instead, he saw a chipmunk scurrying away. Taking a breath and putting the safety back on his mace, he continued his trek into his own personal hell.

He walked for an eternity, his legs killing him soon after, and he had at least thirty bug bites on his body. He glanced down at his watch to see if he should head back to Gina. He'd been away for approximately thirty minutes, and deciding that wasn't enough time to return, he pressed on with slumped shoulders.

Up ahead he saw a rock outcropping and a giant mound of dirt. He thought perhaps someone had been digging, and then thought that perhaps he'd stumbled across the ritual burial site of a serial killer. Would mace be appropriate for a situation like this?

Jake approached slowly. At least murder was something he'd dealt with in his life, or at least read about in the papers every day. When he stood a foot in front of the pile, he saw thousands of ants working together to build the mound. He'd seen anthills before on the discovery channel, but nothing like this.

The mound stood almost five feet in height. Jake thought they were trying to reach for something. He looked up and saw a black mold-like substance on the lowest branch of the tree next to him.

Curious, he reached and touched it and brought his hand down. The stuff was thick and sticky, and when he rubbed his fingers together it flaked off and fell on top of the mound of dirt. The ants stopped what they were doing and began to collect the flakes, taking them down the hole in the center of the mound.

Jake felt a tingling sensation in his fingers, but got distracted by a breeze brushing by and knocking his hat off. At the same moment, several bits of the mold fell from the branch and onto his head. The mold traveled down to his scalp and began to burrow deep into his skin.

He scratched his head for a bit, the itchy and tingling annoying him. After a moment, the itching went away, but so did some of his memories. He automatically placed the hat back on his head.

The mold began to burrow down into the host body's brain. Certain areas were left alone, like the parts controlling breathing, the heart, and other primary bodily functions. This body was much more interesting than the other creatures it had inhabited in the past, and perfect for what needed to be done.

Jake felt something begin to blend with his brain. He could hear its thoughts: *With a body like this within our control, things would move along much quicker.* Jake reached up and grabbed several handfuls of the mold and shoved them into his pockets. He was aware of what he did, he just didn't know why he did it.

He chalked it up to too much fresh air and decided to return to the campsite before anything else weird occurred. During his walk back, he picked up a stick. He thought Gina might like it. She always told him he didn't get her nice things like a normal boy-friend should.

As he neared the campsite, he slowed down and hid behind a bush, peering over it to see Gina. He felt the need to stalk her and make sure she didn't pose a threat to him. He shook his head, wondering where the bizarre thought had come from.

On the ground next to him were some rocks. He picked one up, curious as to what it tasted like. He licked it, then spit out the dirt covering it from his mouth and dropped it. Nature made him do weird things, and he wasn't a fan. Jake felt a ripple across his stomach and thought he must have worked up an appetite with all the hiking.

He walked towards the campsite. The cooler would have food in it to feed his hunger. He walked right by Gina, ignoring her. He opened the cooler and rifled through it.

Jake tossed out hamburger and hot dog buns, soda, ice, and fruit. He smiled when he got to the good stuff: steak and ground beef. Debating between the two for about fifteen seconds, he grabbed one of the steaks and ripped open the package.

"Jake, what are you doing? That's our dinner." Gina stood be-side him, an angry look on her face.

Jake put the steak back in the cooler and reached into his back pocket. He put on his best smile and presented Gina with the stick.

"What the hell is this? You're giving me a stick? What's wrong with you? And look, you've made a mess of everything."

The smile disappeared from his face. Why did he like her again? Somewhere between finding the mold and arriving back at camp, he'd completely forgotten why he loved his girlfriend. She harped on him, nit-picked him, and complained about everything.

"Hey, what smells? It's like something died. God, it's disgusting." She glanced around, sniffed her armpits, then began to lean in and smell Jake. "It's you. What did you get into?"

Some weird instinct made Jake shove his hand into his front pocket, grab some of the mold, which his brain now told him was actually a spore, and smear it on the top of Gina's head.

"Have you lost your mind?" Gina began to shake her head and scratch it.

Jake smiled, and less than a minute later, Gina stopped trying to rip out her hair. She stared at him with a vacant expression. Glancing around the camp, she turned and began to walk east. He had no idea where she was going, and didn't care. All he wanted to do was eat the T-bone he was holding. He brought the steak up to his watering mouth, then ripped into the raw meat, relishing in its taste. He tore every last morsel off the bone, then began to gnaw on it. After he chipped a tooth, he tossed it to the side and reached into the cooler for another one.

Within moments, he'd eaten all of the meat, but the hunger still remained. He knew the spore in his pockets needed to be spread; it wanted new homes all over the world. With Jake's help, and now Gina's as well, it would go much faster.

Jake went to the car, got behind the wheel, and stepped on the gas pedal. The car didn't move, much to his annoyance. He felt the spore digging around in his brain to solve the problem. A flash came to him; something about keys. He reached into his pocket and pulled out an animal foot of some kind with several keys attached to it. He tried to stick them into the A/C adapter until he noticed a slot behind the big round steering wheel.

After several tries, he got the car started. This time when he pressed on the pedal the engine revved loudly, but still didn't move. He glanced down and slapped his forehead, bits of spore flying everywhere. Of course, he needed to put the transmission into gear.

Gina stood in front of the tree. She could see the spore on the branch, but couldn't reach it. She stepped on the mound and the loose soil gave way beneath her. Within seconds she found herself in a pile of dirt and covered in ants.

The tiny stings and bites annoyed her and she tried to wipe the little insects off her. She stood swatting at her body, but the ants kept coming. They were hungry and finally had food. Within seconds they had covered her from head to toe, burrowed into every orifice, and filled her lungs and suffocated her.

Soon, Gina was nothing more than a pile of bones, and several thousand bloated ants roamed around looking for new prey.

They had no need to build anymore; they had attracted what they needed with the other tall human. Now they simply needed to feed.

An hour later, Jake enjoyed the view of civilization as the car crested a hill. Every now and then, he would roll down his window and drop some spore in hopes the wind would carry it somewhere new and exciting.

The hunger had returned, and his craving for flesh was almost debilitating. He pulled over at a gas station. Tumbling out of the car, he assumed he was stiff from sitting for so long. He entered the mini-store to try and find some meat. The best he could find was some stale beef jerky.

He began to walk out of the store with it when the clerk called out to him. "Hey, buddy, you gotta pay for that."

Jake stopped and stared at the man yelling at him. He walked over to the counter, a memory in the back of his head about using paper to get stuff. He pulled out a small leather square from his back pocket and handed it to the man.

The man took it with a questioning look. Jake simply stared at him as he tried to eat the jerky through the plastic wrapper.

"Ah okay, you're special. I get it. Problem is, dude, you don't have any cash so I'm gonna have to charge it on your credit card, okay?" Jake watched as the man took out several pieces of green paper from the leather square and put them into his pocket, then took out several small pieces of plastic as well.

"Okay, the total is five bucks, unless you want gas, too," he said.

Jake looked at the man and nodded. A moment later, a piece of paper appeared in front of him. There were an awful lot of zeroes and part of Jake screamed at himself about being ripped off.

"So, you need to sign this okay? You know how to do that, right?" The clerk gave Jake a condescending smile.

As Jake glanced down at the piece of paper he was supposed to sign, he continued to struggle with the wrapped jerky. He bent down and licked the paper. When he leaned back, he hoped he'd done it correctly.

"Dude, what's wrong with you? You got a seriously disgusting dandruff problem." The clerk grabbed a rag and began clearing away the black flakes coating the counter.

"Look, this is a pen." The man held up what looked like a thin plastic stick. "You use it to sign your name on this." He then held up the paper Jake had licked.

Jake smelled the sweat and blood pumping inside the man across from him. His stomach seized with cramps and he doubled over in pain.

"Hey, dude, you can't die in here, my boss will kill me. Look, just take the jerky and leave."

Jake took the pen and let his eyes roam over the paper. Without hesitation, he reached out and stabbed the man in the eye. Jake didn't like him, nor did the spore taking over his brain. The man backed into the counter behind him, knocking over several magazines as he screamed in pain.

Jake walked around the counter, watching the screaming man. Blood gushed out of his eye, spraying across Jake's face. His tongue darted out and he took a taste. The clerk slipped on the glossy magazines and fell to the floor. Jake descended on him, taking a bite out of his neck.

Jake swallowed the large chunk of flesh without chewing. The cramp in his stomach eased a bit, and he smiled. The clerk tried to defend himself, but Jake grabbed the weakening arms with ease and held them down. The blood flowed freely from the severed carotid artery. Jake leaned in and began to feast on the body in front of him.

He stood moments later and tossed the jerky to the side. He paid no attention to the blood and gore covering him. As he walked back to his car, he knew it needed fuel. At the pumps, several different devices overwhelmed him, but part of him knew he could do this. He grabbed a hose and turned towards the car.

He squeezed the nozzle and poured some gas into the backseat of the car. Something about it seemed wrong so he stopped. He noticed the small square on the side of the car and opened it. A memory came back to him and he knew to put the nozzle in the hole, *after* opening it. He smiled, proud of himself.

When he heard a click, he pulled out the nozzle and left it dangling.

Then got into the car, leaving the gas cap off and lid open. He started the engine and drove towards the city.

The spore in his brain told him to pick a place he could spread it more effectively.

As he cruised along, a honk from behind got his attention. He glanced into the rearview mirror and flinched at what he saw. His skin had a greenish-gray tint to it, and his eyes were losing their color.

The honking continued, taking his attention away from his appearance. The driver in the car behind him raised a finger; a memory flared and Jake stopped the car.

Several cars began to beep, and several fingers and colorful expressions were sent his way. Jake got out of his car and started to walk to the car behind him.

He smiled as the man got out, large and burly, his bearded face red from yelling. Jake wanted to eat him like he'd eaten the clerk, but the spore in his brain told him not to.

"Can't you read the signs? The speed limit is sixty-five, you moron, not forty."

Jake dug deep into his pocket and smeared spore across the angry man's face. In seconds he stopped yelling and began to scratch at his face.

Out of spite to the spore hijacking his brain, Jake leaned in and took a small bite out of the man's arm, then turned around and went back to his car.

"Jesus, you're a freak. I'm calling the cops on you!"

He had a mission to accomplish: *spread the spore*. Jake traveled for another fifteen minutes and reached his final destination. He stared at the building in front of him.

The spore had rooted through Jake's memories and discovered that this was the place to go if he wanted to spread something.

The spore now in control of ninety percent of Jake's thoughts propelled his body forward and into the bus station men's restroom. He took out the remaining spore from his pockets and began to spread them on door handles, faucets, paper towel dispensers, and on top of the toilet seats.

He smiled to himself at his good work; all places in which contact with hands or hair would be likely.

The spore preferred hair on the head as it made burrowing into the brain quicker, but it would take what it could get.

Mike Henderson stood at a urinal, trying not to pay attention to the weirdo coating everything with dust.

He was about to zip up when the man rubbed up against him. He looked down at his shoulder and saw some of the dust on him.

His hands occupied, he tried to clear it off using his chin. That's when it grabbed onto his stubble.

He forgot what he was doing and raised his hands to try and scratch his now itchy chin, but it was too late. The spore began spreading up into his brain.

Mike stood there, unzipped, knowing he had to spread the spore. The only problem was, he didn't have any spore to spread. He looked at the man who'd entered, now recognizing him as a fellow spore spreader.

From the looks of him, he was close to becoming the first spore human hybrid. If not, he would keel over anytime, as he appeared to look dead.

Mike turned and sized up the other men in the bathroom, all of them with vacant expressions on their face. The spore amassed in their brains, telling them what to do. Mike listened to what his spore said.

He turned and walked out of the bathroom, to start his trek to the forest where the tree with the spore stood, still unzipped.

As Mike entered the main area of the bus station, he felt a cramp seize his stomach. He hadn't eaten all day, and all of a sudden the people around him looked appetizing. He began to approach an especially tasty looking woman.

"Oh my God, someone call the police! This guy is a pervert." The woman reached into her bag and pulled out a small bottle.

Mike went in for the kill and felt a stinging sensation in his eyes, as the woman sprayed him with something. Then he felt a pain in his groin which brought him to his knees. He really wished he'd remembered to zip up; she wore a pair of pointed-toe high heels.

He saw the foot lift again to kick him and he grabbed it and bit. After he tasted her, he needed to have more. He held onto her leg, taking chunks out of it as she beat him with her purse. A few moments later, security arrived and took them both away.

Jake watched the men in the bathroom, happy to see he'd spread the spore. Over the course of several minutes, many men entered and left with the spore on them. It burrowed into their brain by any means necessary. Some were infected from sitting on the toilet, and others were invaded through the hands when they touched the taps or handles.

Jake, now fully controlled by the spore, walked out of the bathroom. The cramping in his stomach started again. He needed to eat, and the terminal had many morsels to choose from. He heard a commotion to the side and saw one of the men from the bathroom. Then a woman attacked the man with her bag and security came and took the man away, as well as the woman.

Jake used the distraction to get something to eat. He saw a woman off to the side sleeping on a bench. As he made his way over to her, he ignored the curious glances and outright stares sent his way.

When he sat on the bench next to her, she didn't move. Jake leaned over her and the smell of alcohol and urine almost knocked him out.

He grabbed his stomach as another spasm hit. With a frown, he looked at the nasty, homeless woman and sighed. He closed his eyes and grabbed her by the head, pulling her into a sitting position. Opening his mouth wide, he sank his teeth into her cheek. A patch of leathery skin came off in his teeth and he chewed it, reveling in the fleshy texture.

She didn't scream. Her eyes shot open in shock and she stared at Jake. He had no idea what she saw, but it took the will to live right out of her. As he leaned in to take another bite—this time he felt like eating an eye—he heard her whisper, *"Thank you."*

Jake paid no attention to her, more fascinated by the pop of the little orb in his mouth and the tasty juice squirting out of it. He smiled, and a memory of an expression rose up: too good to eat just one. He extended his tongue again and sucked out the other eye, enjoying the process once more.

All around him, people screamed as they witnessed him eating the woman, but he ignored them.

While in the middle of pulling out a string of intestines like a demented clown's trick hanky, he was pulled from his fun when something hit his shoulder, knocking him to the floor. He turned to look at who would dare to bother him, and saw all hell had broken out while he'd been enjoying his own mini buffet.

Police were everywhere; the men from the bathroom were attacking everyone. Shots were fired haphazardly, which must have been what hit Jake in the shoulder. He peered down and saw the hole, though no blood came out, just some black ooze, and a bit of dust.

The spore in him smiled, which made the muscles on Jake's face smile. He went back to watching the chaotic crowd. One of the men's heads exploded like a rotten melon when a bullet entered his forehead.

The skull splintered apart, brain matter splattering everywhere, along with a large cloud of black dust.

Everyone within a thirty foot radius began scratching as the dust settled on them, then they stopped and joined in on the carnage within seconds.

Interesting, the spore in Jake's head thought. Apparently the spore, when mixed with human DNA, created some sort of thoughtless cannibalistic carrier.

Things would be so much easier now. Jake stood up and walked between the crowd of the infected, and the meals of the infected.

He exited the building and stared at the bright sun, a wide smile on his face. Utter chaos began to rule the streets.

People were covered in blood, and others ran around with random body parts in their hands, while organs dangled from their mouth.

Shots were fired on occasion, and the mushroom cloud of black spore could be seen when bullets hit their mark. The spore would be able to spread over the entire planet within months, maybe even weeks.

Things would be different this time. The humans were easy to take over and open to suggestion upon first contact.

After the humans, there were thousands of animals to move on to. Finally, the spore would have some fun. Jake walked along and pulled off one of his decayed fingers.

Spore started to ooze out of it and he let it leave an inky black trail behind him.

Dr. Virginia Tate stared at the man lying on the gurney in front of her. The emergency room had been overrun with the strangest outbreak she'd ever witnessed.

She removed the cover to see what she was dealing with and noticed he must have been exposing himself, and therefore the woman had beat the hell out of him.

The woman in question laid on the gurney next to the man; she was oddly quiet. Virginia glanced over as a nurse treated the woman for a bite wound.

"Can you tell me your name? What happened? Where are you from?" Virginia tried to talk to the man, but for the last twenty minutes all he'd done was fight against his restraints. Virginia sighed.

The sirens outside were on all the time now, and every off-duty doctor had been called in to help.

Unfortunately, only a handful had answered, and of those only three had made it in. There were rumors swirling around of a possible quarantine.

If it really happened, she knew they were screwed. Government quarantines weren't something to mess around with, and this was no badly-written horror movie.

She needed those blood test results, and until she knew what she was dealing with, she had no way of knowing how to treat the virus.

Antibiotics weren't working, nor were topical creams.

Whatever happened to these people seemed to be causing them to decay at an accelerated rate; it seemed as if they were rotting.

What worried her more was the fact that several of her nurses and interns had gone missing since the arrival of the infected patients.

"Dr. Tate, here are the blood test results," a lab tech said.

Virginia watched the lab technician scurry off after he stole a glance at the man on the gurney.

Virginia read over the results, and then she re-read them. This couldn't be right. According to the results, some sort of fungus or spore had invaded the blood system and was eating the body from the inside out.

"Oh God." She examined the 'rate of growth' and knew they were in trouble.

She ran to her office and locked the door. She withdrew her cell phone and speed dialed the Center for Disease Control. She calculated they had at most forty-eight hours until the entire city would be overrun with spore-infected individuals.

"Hello." The voice sounded gruff and tired.

"Henry, it's Virginia. We have a situation here. I'm sending you some blood test results in case something happens to me."

"Whoa, slow down, Virginia. What are you talking about?"

"It's a damn outbreak of epic proportions, Henry. I've never seen anything like it. In a matter of hours, things have degraded to chaos here. You need to send in a team, but be careful, I haven't figured out how it spreads."

A gunshot out in the hallway caused Virginia to freeze. Through the vent in her office, small bits of dust came in. She began to scratch her head, then stopped.

She dropped the phone, as the voice continued calling out to her.

She needed to spread the spore.

Dr. Henry Cahill regarded the city from inside the helicopter. They'd quarantined the entire city, but he knew the effort was wasted.

Bombs were about to be dropped to eradicate the virus before it got out of control and spread to other states; the entire country.

He held out hope for Virginia, hoping she'd managed to escape, but from what he saw, no one had gotten out alive. Moments later, explosions were heard as the blasts ripped through the city.

Henry stared out the window and watched mushroom clouds appear. In those clouds were dust, and they were heading west with the wind.

Some of the dust even invaded the interior of the helicopter through the vents. Immediately, Henry and the others began scratching their heads, then stopped.

The pilot flying the helicopter stared down at the controls, trying to recall how they all worked.

Well, this would be interesting.

WANTED: THE DESERT'S RELUCTANT DEAD

KATIE SIMMONS

Clay Thompson sat atop his weary, blood-spattered horse as he peered into the vast Arizona night. An eerie silence rang in his ears. There were no howling coyote cries, no pianos plunking show tunes, and none of the usual laughter pouring from the saloons. Everything at this moment seemed calm and right, but Clay still couldn't let his guard down. He sat on high alert, watching for any movement. His ragged hat was pulled low over his eyes, as if he were keeping out the light from a blinding, high-noon sun. In his arms, he cradled his double-barreled shotgun, still smoking from the last blast he'd hammered into the rotted-out skull of a walking dead. A fresh cut on his bicep left a slow stream of blood seeping through his tattered black duster.

As he peered into the dark solitude of the cactus-dotted horizon, he took a long drag from his lit cigarette and exhaled deeply, letting the smoke billow up in a large cloud, like a smoke signal from a native tribe's fire. As he took another drag from his cigarette, he jumped at the startling sound of his horse exhausting its stress from the day's fight.

Clay sat and laughed out loud to himself. His mother had warned him about heading west. She said he wouldn't find a damned thing, nothing but his early grave, a diseased woman, or a scalp-hungry savage.

Well that's a mother for you, he thought to himself. He glanced down at his horse. *Funny thing is I found none of those things. I found something much worse; something incomprehensible.*

He turned to look at the small town situated five hundred feet behind him, sitting in the confinement of the vast lonely desert. Of all the buildings along the main street in town, only one was now lit by a dim oil lamp near the front window. Not a wise thing to do at a time like this, but a necessary move that served as a sign there were still living people in town.

Clay threw his cigarette to the ground and quickly jumped off his horse to stomp the lit butt into the dry desert floor. He took his horse's bridle and pulled its face toward his to look the animal in the eye. "Last thing we need is a fire taking out our shelter, huh boy?" he said. He waited for a second, as if his horse was going to reply. Once he was satisfied that his conversation was definitely one-sided, he shook his head and looked back at the small, dusty town.

"Well, I guess break time's over. It's time to head back." Clay jumped back on his horse and turned it toward town. Slowly and cautiously, he guided the horse through the dark night. He hoped to make it all the way to the safe house without any hair-raising events. He searched the area with a watchful eye, and it appeared that his horse was doing the same. Next to the safety of indoors, out in the open was where Clay preferred to be. He could spot a living corpse much easier than he could amongst the buildings and wooden posts inside the town.

If it was up to him, Clay would have stayed locked up in a building, or would have simply made his way to the high desert where no one would be able to find him. As it was, though, he had to get back to town and join the small group of eight survivors. They were all that remained in the small western town that had been ravaged by a sudden epidemic. It wasn't the normal epidemic, though; this one was darkly different. One that had made the Black Plague look strangely dull. It appeared to be a plague of walking corpses, bodies coming back from the dead after digging themselves free from their graves.

Once Clay reached the main street in town, he picked up the pace a little bit. He always grew nervous when navigating the narrow streets, where a living corpse could be lurking and go undetected till it was too late. Seconds later, Clay reached the Golden Spur Saloon and Gambling Hall where the other survivors were holed up. He jumped off his horse and looked over toward the end of the boardwalk, where a heap of corpses were.

All of them had massive wounds to their heads, either by blunt force, a hatchet, or a bullet. It was the one and only way Clay and the other survivors knew how to stop them. Though he was certain the pile of corpses weren't going anywhere, he was still nervous even standing near them. He was pretty sure they were now *dead*, but over the last couple of days, he started to believe anything was possible.

Unease began to overtake him. He quickly pounded on the door and hollered for someone to let him in. Almost instantly, the doors swung open and a short Japanese man gestured for him to come inside. Clay walked through the door and led his horse in behind him.

"No, no, no," waved the small Japanese man. "The horse can't come in here," he said, pointing to Clay's horse.

Clay briefly looked at his horse, who snorted a sound of disapproval. He appeared to be in deep thought while he patted the horse on the nose before saying aloud, "Thor and I am awful tired of getting chased by the walking dead, and I'm not about to have him eaten by those things. He stays in here with us." Clay looked around and made his voice even louder for all to hear. "Does anyone have a problem with that?" He slammed his shotgun butt down on the floor in emphasis of his firmness on the matter.

Everyone shook their head to show they were all in agreement and turned back to the card games they were playing as Clay led Thor inside. The Japanese man gave a shake of his head, boarded the door back up, and quietly scurried behind the bar. Clay looked at his horse and gave the animal a pat on his head. "There you go, boy. Don't mind that man; he knows who rules this roost."

Thor let out a large puff of air from moist nostrils, as if the horse understood. Clay left Thor standing near the front wall as he went to sit down at a small round table in the middle of the room. He let out a sigh of exhaustion and took his hat from his head, wiping the sweat from his forehead and then repositioning it with the brim low over his eyes. He glanced around the room at the other survivors, wondering if they were at all curious as to what he'd found during his stakeout, if anything.

"Playing cards?" he asked in a surprised tone. "That's what we're doing here tonight? Playing cards?"

"Yeah," said a small boy about the age of nine. "What else is there to do? It isn't safe to go outside with all this going on."

"Ha!" the little boy's grandmother said as she glared at Clay. "It's barely safe in here. Especially when we have a no-good gunslinger who think he owns us all."

"Shhh!" the old woman's daughter snapped. "If it wasn't for Clay, we'd all be dead." She looked at Clay and smiled. "I'm sorry. She's a little out of sorts as of late."

Clay shook his head as if he took no offense to the matter. "That's all right, Maggie. No need to apologize…for others," He gave a smart-ass smile toward the old woman. "Stubbornness sticks hard at that age."

The old woman crumpled her face and let out an angry sigh. She rose from the table and slowly made her way to the bar to join the small Japanese man.

"What can I get you, Evelyn?" the man asked.

Evelyn stared back at the table where Clay and her daughter were now sitting together, chatting happily. She grumbled to herself and turned back around to face the little Japanese man.

"What do you think of that?" she asked with a sour face.

The Japanese man glanced past Evelyn to see what she was talking about. "Oh, I would say that's two people about the same age talking." He paused for a second, then reached for a cup from beneath the bar. He proceeded to fill it with steaming hot coffee. "I would say it's perfectly normal, nothing to worry about."

"Nothing to worry about?" Evelyn said with a huff. "She's too much of a lady for that scoundrel." She paused for a moment to observe how much coffee was being poured into the cup in front of her. "That's enough, Chin," she said with a wave of her hand. "Thank you."

Chin put the coffee pot back behind the counter and turned his attention back to Clay and Maggie. "I'd agree that Maggie seems like a fine lady, but I've known Clay for a while and he's a pretty decent guy."

"Decent out here doesn't mean much if you ask me," Evelyn said. "He probably doesn't even know how to carry on a respectable conversation with a woman."

"He was married before, you know," Chin said.

Evelyn looked at him and shook her head. "You're fooling me."

"No ma'am," he said in all seriousness.

"Ah," sighed Evelyn. "Was it a real marriage or one of those live in types?"

"It was real. They were married for about a year before she died."

Evelyn, being stubborn and not wanting to believe there was any good in Clay, still shook her head in disbelief. "I'm sure she wasn't too much of a catch herself then."

"You couldn't be more wrong," Chin argued. "She was a school teacher, an active part in the community and just about the nicest woman you could ever have met. I expect they did well for one another, being opposite in that matter."

"I suppose you're right," Evelyn agreed. "Still, I don't like it one bit, the idea of my daughter taking a liking to that man."

"Relax," Chin said. "It's not like they have much choice. The choice in people you can converse with nowadays has been drastically cut down."

Clay glared over at Evelyn and Chin. "I think they're talking about me again," he said to Maggie.

Maggie turned to look at her mother and Chin. "I expect you're right."

Clay's attention shifted to Maggie's son James, who had been staring at Clay's horse.

"What's the matter, James?" Clay asked.

James scrunched up his nose and sighed. "Why do you call your horse Thor?"

"Well, what am I suppose to call him?"

"I don't know. Maybe something like Flash, Thunder, or Lightning."

"Well, Thor does mean thunder in the Norse language," Clay explained.

"So, you did name him after thunder?" James asked in an excited tone.

"Not exactly. His name was originally Jake when I bought him from a friend, but after he got me through some tough times I renamed him Thor. This comes from the Norse God of strength, thunder and war. He's just about the strongest animal I've ever seen emotionally and physically."

James looked at him as if he had a screw loose. "Then why don't you keep him outside, if he's so strong? He could fend off those dead people that're out walkin' the streets."

"I don't think Thor would have that easy of a time," Clay said. "Besides, he's all I have left. If anything happened to him, I'd lose my mind. I want him near me so we can keep an eye on one another." He played with the gold ring he wore on his right ring finger.

"What's that?" James asked.

"Hush, James," Maggie hissed.

"It's all right," Clay said.

Clay took the ring off and twisted it around in his fingers. "It's my wedding ring."

"You were married?" James asked.

"Yes, I was."

"Where is she?"

"She died a few months back, of a bad fever," Clay said in a sad tone.

"You miss her?" James continued on, clearly not giving up on the subject.

Clay put the ring back on his finger and managed to give James a slight nod. Then he stood up and slowly walked across the room to be by himself.

Maggie realized James had upset Clay. "Go to bed," she whispered. "I'll be in shortly to tuck you in."

James looked over at Clay, who was now sitting on a bar stool across the room by himself. He realized he'd upset Clay, too. "I didn't mean to upset him, Mama."

"I know you didn't, honey. Just go to bed." She kissed him on the forehead.

Once James scurried across the floor and had closed the door to the back room, where the beds were set up, Maggie glanced over toward Clay.

She took a deep breath and made her way over to try and talk to him. "Do you mind if I sit here?"

Clay patted the stool with a lethargic passion. "Be my guest."

Maggie sat down and sighed awkwardly. "I'm sorry about that. He doesn't understand."

"Don't worry about it," Clay said quickly, cutting her off.

"Oh, that's right. I shouldn't apologize for other people." She smiled slightly.

Clay ignored the comment for a second, then turned to face her. "You know, I do miss her terribly. I can't stand it some days. For those first couple of months after she died, when I realized I'd never see her again, I'd lay awake almost every night wishing she was still with me. I was terrified of going to sleep. I thought that for every night I fell asleep, her face would be erased a little each time from my memory. Each night lurked the question of: *When I awake, will I still remember her face?* But I'm no longer scared of that."

"That's good, isn't it?" Maggie asked.

Clay looked away and shook his head. He let out a deep sigh, which turned into a cough as he tried to choke back his emotions. "No." As he turned to face her once more, Maggie could see his eyes glazing over. "Now, I'm scared that I'll see her face again…" He nodded his head in the direction of the front door. "As one of them." Maggie looked at the door as if something was coming through it. She turned away and shook her head and thought of something to say to make him feel better. "I wouldn't worry about that, Clay. My father, James' grandfather, died about seven months ago. We took a visit to his grave the other night, and he's still there. The way I figure it, these corpses that're comin' back to life and roamin' around, they've been dead for a while. If he's still buried, I'm sure she is, too."

Clay took a shot of whiskey and hissed at its bitterness. "I'm not sure if that's really a help or not."

Maggie looked away for a second, ashamed of herself.

"Although," Clay said quickly. "It does comfort me a bit. Maybe we can figure out what's going on before time gets to her, too."

"I sure hope so," Maggie agreed.

He looked at her and smiled, then looked away, "I hope for your sake, too. I bet it wouldn't be easy to have seen your father like that."

"Oh, I don't care about that," she shrugged. "He deserved the first death he got. He wasn't a very good person."

He wasn't sure what to say in response to that. The small gesture Maggie made to try and comfort him made Clay feel a little better, as strange as it sounded. He sat there with her for a minute, as they drank their beverages slowly; enjoying the peace and quiet they hadn't been able to enjoy very much the last few days. They thought that perhaps it was over. The last living dead that was encountered was hours ago. Other than that, activity had died down considerably.

Unfortunately, a few minutes later, they were proven wrong. Everyone in the room jumped up and let out a quick gasp as they heard pounding coming from outside the saloon.

"Wait here," Clay said, as he grabbed a revolver from the bar top and headed to the door. "Chin, follow me and secure the door behind me. I'll let you know when it's safe to let me back in."

Chin quickly made his way around the bar and followed cautiously behind Clay till he reached the door. Clay slowly cracked the door open and immediately fired a shot into the skull of a walking dead that was slowly meandering up the two rickety wooden steps to the saloon's boardwalk. Clay poked his head outside to get a better look of the surroundings. He looked to his left and immediately pulled back inside, slamming and securing the door again.

He raced over to the bar with Chin following nervously behind.

"What is it?" Chin asked frantically. "What did you see?"

Clay reached behind the bar and grabbed more guns and ammunition. "Well, they're back again," Clay said in a forced, calm tone, trying to hide the need to panic.

"What do you mean 'they're back again'?" Maggie asked as the others got up and walked over to the bar to join him.

"You know how we thought damage to the brain would do it?" he asked.

"Yeah," they all said in unison.

Clay stopped messing with the guns for a moment. "That didn't work," he said bluntly, then returned to loading more guns.

Rob, a man about Clay's age with the same talent for shooting, stepped forward and spat a large wad of chew into a nearby spittoon. "Let me get this straight," Rob said. "What you're sayin' is that all those dead bastards who came back to life so to speak, and who we killed for a second time, came back to life yet again?"

"Precisely," Clay nodded.

"How the hell are we supposed to get rid of 'em?" Rob asked, as he stared around the room, looking for someone who could offer up an answer.

"There are other ways to do things like that," Joseph said, an old veteran of war.

"Like what, old man?" Rob asked in a disrespectful tone.

"I'll tell you as soon as you wipe that smart-ass look from your face, young man," Joseph said.

Rob did as he was told and grew quiet long enough for Joseph to explain. "The least dangerous option for the town, and one that's not as messy, would be to keep doin' what we're doin'," Joseph said.

"Obviously that doesn't work," Rob said angrily.

"It buys us time," Joseph snapped.

"All right, settle down there, you two," Clay said. "We don't need to start any wars in here, that's for sure. Now, you both have a point. Joseph, what were your other ideas?"

Joseph sneered at Rob before continuing. "As I was sayin'. Doin' what we've been doin' buys us some time. Those bodies out there that came back to life for a second time were killed a few days ago, so I'm thinkin' we can keep doin' that until we figure this out."

"How're we ever going to figure this out?" Chin asked. "Besides, ammo isn't endless, you know, we can't keep doing this forever."

"True," Joseph agreed. "One of the other options would be dismemberment. I'd imagine if they still managed to come back when they were all cut up, at least they wouldn't be able to do much harm."

"Hmm," Clay sighed "You're right about that one being messy. What was the option that would be dangerous to the town?" he asked.

"Burning them; giving no substance to their soul. They can't attack you if their bodies don't exist. Their souls will just float away with the smoke caused from their rotted-out bodies."

"Gross," Maggie said quietly. "Why don't we just shoot them in the head a few more times, decapitate them, remove their arms and legs and then burn them to ashes?"

The room fell silent and they all turned to look at her inquisitively, dumbfounded by the words coming from such a reserved lady.

"What?" she asked with a shrug. "I was only joking."

"You may have a point there," Rob said, all for the idea.

"It's a good point," Clay said. "But Joseph is right; that's dangerous. We don't want to risk burning down the whole town, especially if there's more of them out there. We might be able to rid the town of the couple hundred that are layin' around the streets, but that doesn't mean more won't be coming our way. Who knows what lies beyond those mountains? Who knows how far this thing has spread?"

"I could care less," Rob said loudly and pointed at the door. "Do you hear that out there? That's the sound of a dozen half-dead living bodies that want to come in here, eat our flesh, and turn us into walking corpses just like them. We better act soon, or at least shoot them now to shut them the hell up. Their groans are givin' me the creeps."

Clay tossed him a gun. "Follow me then," he demanded.

Clay and Rob made their way to the front door with guns in hand. Clay was calm and determined, but Rob was eager, with hatred in his eyes, thirsty for another kill. Before Clay opened the door, he turned to Rob and said, "Keep your head on straight. Between the two of us we have twenty-four bullets and that won't get us very far if you're shootin' poorly."

Rob looked at him sourly. "I've killed more of those things than you have."

Clay pressed his back against the door and lifted his guns in the air, ready to make his move. "I'm not sure that's a valid point here," he said sternly. "After all, they were able to come back to life even with a few bullets to the brain."

Thor snorted loudly and brushed up against Clay's face, anxious to follow.

"Not now," Clay said. "I'll need you later I'm sure, but for now you stay inside where it's safe and get some rest." The horse backed off, as if it understood its master.

Rob sneered and got ready to lunge forward out the door with Clay as soon as he made the move. Clay pushed the door open, and he and Rob dashed onto the boardwalk, Chin quickly boarding up the door behind them.

As soon as the two men were outside, they went low and began firing rapidly, taking down body after body. From inside the safety of the saloon, the others listened in horror at the sound of feet scraping past the door, groans and growls echoing through the night, and shots being fired one after another, followed by the loud thuds of decaying bodies hitting the ground like slabs of beef.

Each shot from Clay and Rob sent blood squirting ferociously from the walking dead. With the last gunshot fired, the groans finally ceased until nothing but silence filled the night. The two men stood still, their breathing heavy, as if they'd been in a strenuous fight.

"Let's get these things cleared away from the door," Clay said. "Be careful to stay away from their mouths, you can't trust these sons-of-bitches."

They began clearing the bodies off to the side.

"Hopefully they'll stay dead this time," Rob said.

When they were finally done piling the bodies, they wiped the sweat from their foreheads and returned to the saloon. As Clay pounded on the door, and Chin opened it, another thud rang out from nearby. Clay turned to see where the noise was coming from, "Shit! Shut the door! More are comin' our way!"

Chin quickly closed the door as Clay turned to see another group of walking dead coming his way. He squinted through the darkness of the night to see them better. "Looks like a fresh batch," he said.

"I'm not sure if that's a good thing or not," Rob added, as he reloaded each of his revolvers.

"I don't think anything about this could be seen as good," Clay said, as he followed suit and reloaded his own guns.

"Well," Rob sighed, slamming both gun chambers closed. "At least, we're using our bullets on fresh ones this time. It seems like such a waste to be shootin' somethin' that had already been killed twice."

Clay laughed. "These may be fresh ones, but they've still been dead for a while. I never thought I'd see the day where I had to use bullets on a dead man, let alone hundreds of 'em."

"Yeah," Rob agreed. The two men were finally agreeing on something. "Maybe we should find a way to tame these things. I'd imagine they'd be good in war."

"I don't know about that," Clay said.

Their conversation was cut short as they noticed another group of dead coming down the other end of the street.

"All right," Clay said, sounding a bit discouraged. "What side do you want to take?"

"It doesn't matter to me," Rob said, as he walked down into the street with Clay. "As long as we start shootin' now and don't let them get any closer."

Rob and Clay both stood their ground in the middle of the street outside the saloon. The moon and a few lampposts that remained lit was the only illumination. Both men had been in-volved in shoot-outs before, but none like this. On opposite sides of the dirt street, separate groups of five to ten walking dead stumbled toward them, kicking up clouds of dust as they moved down the dusty road, moving like a lethargic but steady stampede of undead cannibals. Clay and Rob wasted no time, and they both started to fire rapidly, taking the dead down two at a time. The shooting stopped nearly as soon as it started. When it looked clear, they quickly reloaded, in case more were headed their way from around the alleys connected to the street.

Clay walked down the road to the new pile of corpses he'd created. As he observed the small remains of skin clinging tightly to the skeleton frames, something caught his eye.

Rob also stared down at the pile of bodies, but the snapping of Clay's fingers to get his attention made Rob turn around.

Clay motioned for Rob to come and join him as he stared down at the group of mangled bodies.

Rob rushed over and stood by his side. "What is it?" He was short of breath.

"Take a look at their necks," Clay said.

Rob bent down to get a closer look at what Clay was referring to. On most of the bodies' necks, there was a noticeable mark that was worn away on the flesh.

"What is it?" Rob asked, standing upright again. "Rope burn?" He looked around at the other bodies to see that they didn't have the same mark, though they seemed to have old bullet wounds, suggesting they were involved in criminal activity before their true death.

"Take a look at the others," Clay said. "Something tells me that all these men deserved the early deaths they received. But what brought them back?"

As Rob thought about it, he realized that most, if not all of the walking dead, were sporting wounds that had been inflicted while they were still alive. The more he thought about it, the ones with the strange marks around their necks did seem to walk with their necks hanging limp on their shoulders, as if a broken neck had been the cause of their deaths.

"I don't think these men died of natural causes or old age," Rob said suspiciously.

"Agreed," Clay replied. "It looks like we're fighting some of the most wanted men in the West."

"Oh, that's just perfect," Rob scoffed. "These bastards did all their murdering and stealing before their death, and now hell has spat them back out to give us more of their fury." He glanced at Clay to see what the man's opinion was on the matter.

A warm breeze swept over the two men and sent dust from the street flying into the air. Clay didn't say anything, he just stared off into the distance at an approaching storm outside of town. He watched as the lightning struck the ground in piercing bolts that streaked across the sky in all directions, and felt the rumble of the distant thunder as it sent shock waves down the narrow street, shaking the glass windows and rattling the lampposts.

"I'm convinced there's a reason behind what's going on here, something we can get an answer too. But where?" Clay asked, looking at Rob.

"No idea," Rob said. "But I do think we should go back inside. I'm out of bullets."

"Yeah, me too," Clay added, as he examined his empty chambers. "Let's not share with the others what we found here. There's no need to get them even more panicked."

They turned and headed back to the salon, leaving the dead where they'd fallen.

Rob and Clay entered the safety of the saloon and the door was closed and boarded again. The other survivors stood watching, thankful it was over, for the time being anyway.

James standing by the door leading to the beds in his nightgown, with tears in his eyes. Maggie saw him and went rushing over to him, with the others following behind. "Go back to bed, dear, everything's fine now," she said softly.

"Not everything," James said, in a shaky voice.

"Well, no, not exactly," Maggie said softly. "I'm sure there's more out there, but for now it is all clear."

"No it's not," James said. His eyes began to tear more rapidly.

"What's the matter?" Maggie asked, still holding her son's shoulders, which now began to shake.

"I saw one outside my window," he said, his eyes wide and filled with fear.

Maggie turned to Clay, who knew what he had to do. Once more he and Rob went to the door. It appeared a new batch was coming in. As Clay strode across the room, he could still hear James and Maggie talking.

"James," Maggie said. "It's okay, Clay and Rob will get the bad man."

"But," James said hesitantly. "It's Grandpa."

Clay stopped suddenly and turned to look at Maggie. A chill of fear crept down his spine as he recalled the conversation he and Maggie had had earlier.

By the look on Clay's face, Maggie knew what he was thinking; his wife might be making an appearance next.

Clay stood stiff as a board, unable to move.

"Rob," Maggie said. "Would you please go out and take care of my father?"

Rob tipped his hat and cocked his guns. "I'm on it." He made his way out the door, Chin there to close it after him.

Seconds later, gunshots rang through the night, bringing Clay back to reality. He remembered that Maggie's father had been a man of low moral character and recalled what he and Rob had discovered. He felt a little relieved in believing that there was a very good chance his wife would remain resting in peace; unless she'd done something awful during her time on Earth that he was unaware of. He looked around the room and realized they were one man short. "Where's Joseph?" he asked.

"He followed you two outside a minute after you left. He said he had to do something important. He hasn't come back yet," Chin said.

Suddenly, they heard another gunshot echo in the night. They all looked around nervously at the realization that Joseph was still out there. "I better go help him," Clay said. Chin followed Clay to the door and secured it behind the man.

Clay ran around the side of the building into the dark alley to see Rob standing across from a crowd of walking dead, about ten of them, bearing down on him.

"I got your back!" Clay hollered and joined Rob. They continued shooting, knocking down each of the walking dead like lumber jacks cutting down trees.

When all the dead had been brought down, the two men gathered up the bodies into another pile at the end of the alley. When they were finished, they rested, catching their breath and wiping the dust and sweat from their brows.

"Didn't we just do this?" Rob asked with a slight smirk.

Clay nodded with a half smile. "I'm beginning to think the rest of my life is gonna consist of shooting living corpses, piling up their bodies, and then wiping the sweat from my face that's formed because of the godforsaken heat in this place."

"Listen, what's that?" Rob asked abruptly. "Do you hear that?"

Clay stopped and listened intently and soon began to hear the beating of hooves gradually growing louder. "It's a horse," he said happily.

They ran around the corner of the alley and saw a horse and rider approaching them at full speed. "It's Joseph!" Clay exclaimed, happy to see their friend again.

Joseph reached them but didn't stop, he just slowly trotted by. "Come on," he said. "I found somethin' out."

Clay and Rob followed behind at a quick pace down the dark alley and around the bend to the front of the saloon. Clay pounded on the door and Chin quickly let them inside.

"Oh, come on," Chin sighed as he stared face to face with Joseph's horse. "Another horse? Why can't we leave them outside? They keep shittin' in here and it smells."

"Because they're our main means of survival. Can you run as fast as a horse?" Joseph asked Chin.

The man just shook his head, grumbled and went to go sit down at a nearby table.

"Did you find anything out?" Maggie asked.

"I did," Joseph said. "Everyone gather 'round." "We have some work to do."

Once everyone was seated at the small tables, he began to tell of what he found when he went looking for answers. "I have some great news, followed by some bad news and even worse news."

"All right," Clay said "Tell us the good news first."

"Yes," Evelyn chimed in. "As long as the bad news and even worse news isn't going to stop us from accomplishing the good news."

Joseph nodded, took a drink and said, "I went to the other neighboring towns and they were all deserted. I then decided to go into Apache territory."

"What!" Evelyn yelled. "That's even worse than being out there with the living corpses."

"Not in times like these," Clay remarked.

"Anyhow," Joseph continued. "I decided if anyone would have a clue about this supernatural spooky stuff it would be them, and I was right. On any other given day I would've gotten an arrow through the chest before I spotted a member of their tribe, but given the special circumstances, I was welcomed."

"Are they okay?" Maggie asked.

"Oh yeah," Joseph said. "They're fine. After meeting with the newly appointed chief, I was told a tale that has lived on through their many generations. It was of a curse that was to be placed on the white men for the genocide they'd carried out on the Apache people; a curse in which all white men would come back from the dead and attack their own. What's worse is that the people sent back to *hunt* the living were those that had committed the cruelest of crimes toward mankind during their time on Earth. "

"That's lovely," Evelyn scoffed.

"So this curse is the reasoning for what's occurrin'. The chief informed me that this was an old curse and it was set to take place at the height of this very settlement's population. As it took off it would grow and spread to other parts of the country. To me that sounded good, that means the other parts of the country are fine for now. But that don't mean it'll stay that way. We have to stop what's goin' on here before it spreads."

"Do you know how we can stop it?" Clay asked.

"The ones we already killed came back once more," Maggie added.

"Hmm," Joseph sighed. "Then we don't have much time. The Apache chief told me that according to the legend, they'll keep comin' back. Each time death and rebirth occurs, the time spent in death is shortened until they stay as the livin' in which there is no gettin' rid of 'em for good. The only way to get rid of them is to burn 'em."

"Aha!" Rob exclaimed. "Let's do it now!"

"Not so fast," Joseph said. "The only way it'll work is if we have them all, and burn 'em all at once."

They all fell silent, realizing the enormous and seemingly impossible task at hand.

"I'm not sure if that's possible," Clay said. "How do we know how many there are?"

"I don't think it'll be too difficult," Joseph said. "From what I understand, it's only the ones that came out of their graves already. It's not like we have to wait around for more to unearth themselves, and it's *only* the ones who came from the ground, not those who were killed by them and came back as the same monsters. We already have a head start. We have six big piles scattered around town. We just have to gather ';em all up, throw 'em in a ditch, and burn the bastards."

"Well, if that's what we have to do, I guess that's that," Clay said.

"Yeah," Joseph said. "We don't have a choice."

Clay looked at the others. "Joseph, Rob and I will go around and gather up the bodies. We can each take a wagon. The rest of you, find a shovel and I want you to start digging a ditch out front."

"Yeah," Joseph said. "Make it a big ditch, too. We have a lot of bodies to toss in there."

Everyone knew what their job was going to be, and all knew the struggle they were in for. They knew it was going to be tough, and every single one of them was terrified, stunned and completely unsure of how they were going to do it all in a matter of hours, before the curse became permanent and before the storm hit, making a fire difficult.

As they gathered up the tools necessary for their specific duty, all were silent. It was if they were heading into a line of fire, ready to be killed at any instant. In a sense they were heading for their doom, but they had a chance to change their destiny and make life only for the living, as it was intended to be. The rest of the country knew nothing of the struggle they were about to face and just how much they were sacrificing, and even if they lived to tell the rest of the world about it, no one would believe them.

"All right," Clay said. "My team is ready." He looked at Chin. "You ready with your team?"

Chin nodded.

"Good," Clay replied. "Are we all set on what needs to be done?"

Everyone nodded and said they were.

"Okay then," Clay said with a smile. "Let's do this."

Like bees swarming out of their hive to collect honey for the nest, they all went their separate ways, gathering bodies and digging a large ditch. Clay, Joseph and Rob all headed out on empty wagons to collect the piles of dead bodies that were scattered around town. Maggie, Evelyn, Chin, Joseph and even James all dug endlessly. They dug in silence. Each of them were lost in their own thoughts, worries and concerns until Evelyn spoke up. "Do you think that scoundrel Clay will ruin this for us?" she asked.

"Mother!" Maggie exclaimed. "What's your problem with him? He's done nothing but help us."

"Yeah, well," Evelyn scoffed. "I don't think he's helping us on his own accord, he needs us as much as we need him. That doesn't mean he likes sticking around."

"Evelyn," Chin said as he heaved a heavy shovelful of dirt over his shoulder. "I told you before; he's a good man, just a little rough around the edges."

"Rough around the edges is right," Evelyn said. "I never saw a man take to killing so easily in my life."

"We're all doing things out of the ordinary," Maggie said in an agitated tone.

Evelyn stopped for a second and looked at Maggie. "What was that all about earlier when your father came back? Why did Clay look so shocked?"

"Keep shoveling, and mind your own business for once," Maggie snapped.

Evelyn went back to shoveling but didn't stop her tongue. "This *is* my business; it's all of our business."

"If you must know," Maggie said. "He was worried that his wife would come back and he'd have to kill her, but now that we know it's only the wrong doers that are coming back, he doesn't have to worry."

Evelyn looked over at Chin and said, "I guess now we'll find out for sure how wonderful of a woman his wife really was."

Meanwhile, Clay was moving down yet another dark alley, the only light being provided by the small gas lampposts, the moon, and the distant lightning. With his horse, Thor, he'd been gone for thirty minutes already and had collected over twenty bodies. Thor proudly pushed on as the wagon the horse pulled got heavier with each corpse that was thrown on the pile. Clay pushed on, too, his back feeling the burden of all the heavy lifting he was doing. Some of the older corpses were smaller framed and easier to lift, but some were big-boned and had started to put some stress on his aging back.

As Clay made his way down the last road on the route, he could see an animated corpse up ahead. It was moving around in an almost living fashion, to where he didn't believe it was one of the walking dead, but rather a living person that was injured.

"Hello there!" he called out, hoping for a response.

The figure stopped and turned in his direction, but didn't make a sound. As the figure turned to face him, Clay saw that it was wearing a flowing white gown and the woman's face was too pale to be a living person. His heart nearly stopped. The hair on his arms shot straight up like cactus needles as a chill flooded through him. His heart began to pound and he felt weak.

Could this be my wife? he wondered. But it couldn't be her, because she'd done nothing to deserve such a cruel fate; still he was uneasy.

His heart began to beat so rapidly he feared he would die right on the spot, but despite the quickness of his heart, neither his legs nor arms would move. He remained frozen atop the wagon, just staring at the figure.

Suddenly, the dead woman picked up the pace and began to walk quickly down the dark alley toward him. Clay's eyes began to fill with tears as the figure got closer and he saw hair that resembled his wife's.

Clay raised the gun hesitantly, not wanting to shoot, but knowing he had to. He closed his eyes, not wanting to see the bullet enter the head and the dark blood spurting in all directions. He fired one shot and opened his eyes once the report had faded away, then he hopped down off the wagon and slowly made his way to the crumpled body lying in the dirt.

As he stood over the body, he wiped his eyes and turned the body over to see its face. He let out a huge sigh of relief when he realized it wasn't her. He was able to escape his fear for now; he just hoped the curse could be ended before she made an appearance; if she was going to make one. He didn't believe she would, but he feared that perhaps she had done something in her life that she'd managed to keep hidden from all those who knew her. The Lord knew that Clay had made some mistakes in his life. He only wondered what this woman could have done to have brought her such a cruel fate.

Clay knew time was running out. He cleared his throat and quickly gathered up the corpse, carrying it to the rear of the wagon, and tossing it atop the pile. Then he jumped back on the wagon and joined the others.

Clay finally made it back to the main street and he could see he was the slowest of the group to return with his delivery of bodies to throw into the pit. It was a strange scene to approach; to see a group of people throwing dead bodies into a ditch in the middle of the street. It was a scene Clay hoped to never see again.

"What took you so long?" Evelyn asked in a frantic voice. "They started to come back again."

"It's okay," Chin said. "We got them all."

"Just help me unload them, will you?" Clay asked to his pile of bodies.

They all hopped up onto the wagon and began tossing the bodies into the ditch. They gave no thought to the fact that these were once humans. When they finally threw the last one in, the pile of bodies had reached well over the walls of the ditch.

"That'll have to do," Clay said. "We can't waste any more time."

Chin, who was rolling up torches, lit the end of one and motioned for everyone to grab one and light theirs off of his. When they all held a lit torch, they gathered around the pile of bodies in a circular fashion. They stood silently, watching the enormous pile of decaying, bloody bodies that lay before them as the light from their torches danced around on their faces. None of them could believe this was real, that this pile of hideous creatures had once been people just like them.

"Should we say something?" James asked. "Like we did at Grandpa's funeral?"

They looked at each other, not knowing what to say, and more importantly, not wanting to wait a second longer.

Clay raised his torch high in the air. "Do it!" he yelled. He tossed his flaming torch onto the pile of bodies, and everyone else quickly followed. Almost immediately, the dry clothes of the corpses caught fire.

The group watched as the crackling embers grew brighter and more of the bodies caught fire, the rotting flesh burning and sizzling.

The smell was terrible, beyond anything they ever could have imagined. Each one of them was nauseated beyond belief, coughing and heaving into their arms as they tried to block the stench from hitting their noses.

They weren't sure if it was because of the smell, the sight or the thoughts they were consumed with. There was no way to know if it was officially over. All they knew was they were terrified as hell to turn around, for fear they had missed one. That single straggler would keep the curse spreading and continuing on for eternity.

MILE HIGH

REBECCA SNOW

Chris DeGonia checked his watch. Another fifteen minutes had passed, and the line had inched forward only three feet. At the present rate, he'd make it to the gate by the time the plane reached its final destination.

Three uniformed security officers sauntered past on the other side of the partition, heading for the already clogged checkpoint. They flashed their badges and exchanged pleasantries with co-workers before firing up a new checking station and calling the next hopeful passenger.

Chris shuffled ahead as the line reformed with people scurrying to make it through airport protocol a few seconds faster.

"Do you believe this crap?" a man behind Chris asked, motioning ahead with his chin to the crowd. "You'd think they'd come up with a better way to confiscate my tweezers. Especially for the price they want for tickets and parking."

Chris turned to see a man in a rumpled business suit, a loosened tie hanging on his too-small frame. A pair of wire-rimmed glasses with tape on them sat perched on his beakish nose. The little man shuffled from foot to foot and exchanged a battered, brown briefcase for a trench coat folded over his other arm. Chris smirked and gave a noncommittal shrug before returning to face the backs of everyone in front of him.

"The least they could do is get more people to work the scanners," the man continued to grumble as the line crept forward.

"Please take off your shoes and place them in the bins provided," a woman called, as she replenished a stack of tan containers so high they were about to topple. "Any loose items, place them in a bin."

Chris slipped out of his short boots and wiggled his sock-covered toes, before tossing his footwear into a receptacle, along with his red travel pillow, cell phone and wallet. He placed his black carry-on bag on the belt and watched as it rode the conveyor into the darkened X-ray tunnel.

"Any jackets, please take them off and place them in the bin," the woman's voice droned behind him.

Chris stepped toward the metal detector and stood on the mat to wait. One of the female officers took his ticket and identification. She glanced at the photo on his license and then at his face before passing it back to him.

"Step through," she said.

He emerged without hearing the disheartening beep as his shoes reappeared from under the rubber flap. Tossing his boots to the floor, he stepped into them. He stuffed his wallet in a pocket, then tucked the pillow under his arm. Weaving away from the flow of foot traffic, he stood at the end of the belt and waited for his bag to materialize.

He glanced down and noticed his boot laces splayed across the carpet. As he squatted down to tie them, he saw the technician scan his bag a second time. He guessed that the keystrokes meant they were zooming in on his MP3 player, so he yanked the strings and stood. The man pointed to the screen and nodded before sending out the piece of luggage.

A scuffle erupted in the next line. Chris swung his wheeled bag from the platform and lengthened the handle so the bag could roll behind him as he walked down the crowded corridor. He glanced at his watch. As he began to run, he heard a scream from the line.

"Some people just can't deal with people pawing through their drawers," Chris mumbled while jogging to the gate.

The yelling behind him continued, but as he distanced himself from the turmoil, the heightened pitch lessened. People he passed turned to stare through the mass of bodies. Some of them looked at him as if he'd caused the commotion. He kept pace as he ran to his plane. The line at gate seventeen had dwindled to only one man and the flight attendants when Chris trotted to a stop and huffed to catch his breath.

"Flight four-eighty-two?" he asked, handing the woman his ticket to scan.

"You made it just in time," she nodded, then ran the barcoded paper under her handheld laser scanner.

Chris smiled and retrieved his ticket before jostling his baggage over the threshold to the hallway.

"Am I too late?" another man asked, gasping at the stewardess. "There was a huge mess at the screening area."

Chris slowed his steps to listen.

"No, sir," the feminine voice said. "Oh, you're bleeding. Do you need a doctor?"

"Just a scratch," the man said. "Some nutjob hadn't taken his meds and was biting people. He only nipped me, though."

Chris stopped dead in his tracks.

"When we get on board, we'll get you cleaned up and bandaged," she said.

Footsteps approached, and Chris took a tentative step as the other man brushed past him, carrying a leather jacket and backpack.

"Excuse me," Chris called. "Did you say someone bit you?"

The man spun and walked backwards. Even at six foot two, Chris had to look up to meet his eyes.

"Yeah, can you believe this crap?" He held up his bleeding hand as proof. "They got the guy down with a taser, but he was still struggling. They wanted me to make a statement, but the place went nuts, so I just slipped out to make the flight." He coughed and slowed, turning to walk beside Chris. "That guy chewed on enough other people that they didn't need me for proof, too."

Chris and the man reached the gangplank just as the flight attendant appeared behind them.

"We hope you enjoy your flight. Please find your seats, and we'll be on our way," she said with a wide smile that showed off her perfect teeth.

Chris and the man shuffled through the aisle as the other passengers stowed their carry-on bags and settled into their seats. As the airline was fully booked and didn't assign seats, the only two spots remaining were across the small walkway from the miniscule lavatory.

"Great," Chris muttered. He opened the bin above only to find it already full.

"Do you mind taking the window?" the other man asked. "I'm too big to fit."

Chris sighed. The man wasn't lying. He was taller and wider than Chris, but the window seat meant that Chris would have to fold himself up like a pretzel in order to sit. He tossed his travel pillow onto the seat by the window.

"Sure," he said. "I just need to find a bin for my bag." He retrieved his music player from the case's outer pocket before moving back up the aisle to find an open compartment. Three quarters of the way to the front of the plane, he found an empty space. Hefting his luggage, he shoved it into the hole before returning to his seat unburdened.

Chris nodded to the man standing at the end of the aisle, half inside the bathroom stall. Chris squeezed into the blue-upholstered cushion and twisted to find the seatbelt. When he straightened, he found the other man looking at him.

"I'm Seth. Since we'll be here for a few hours, I thought I'd introduce myself." He plunged his hand forward. A stream of blood dripped onto Chris' pants as he gaped at the bite mark on Seth's arm.

Seth pulled away and flinched. "Aw, man. I'm sorry about that." He reached across the walkway, grabbed a handful of paper towels from the restroom, and blotted at the spreading red stain.

Chris swatted at Seth's hands and sighed.

"Here," Seth said, standing as far as the cabin would allow. He pulled a few bills from his wallet. "This should cover the cleaning bill."

Chris looked down at the wad of money and shook his head. "That's okay. I always wear my old pants to fly." He retrieved the discarded, balled-up paper towels and dabbed at his pants. "I'll just toss them when I get home. I'm Chris, by the way."

Seth smiled and slid the money back into his wallet. He squatted and belted himself into his seat before stretching his legs into the aisle. The flight attendant that had greeted them at the door strode toward them, carrying a few first aid supplies. Chris read *Tammy* on her nametag.

"Here you are, sir." She handed Seth some alcohol wipes and a few bandages. "If you need anything else, let me know."

Without waiting for an answer, she spun around and trotted up the aisle to illustrate the use of the oxygen masks and seatbelts as the other flight attendant mumbled into the microphone. Seth craned his neck to watch her retreating, admiring her backside. Tammy glanced back and flashed a wicked grin.

"I think I might need something else about a mile high," Seth said, nudging Chris' elbow off the armrest. He tore one of the foil packets open with his teeth and pressed the small pad to his bleeding arm. He hissed through a clenched jaw. "Is this alcohol or acid?"

By the time the plane taxied down the runway, the small pads lay scattered like red confetti around Seth's shoes. The wound dripped into the upholstery.

"Does it look like it's going to bleed much more?" Seth asked, holding his arm up for Chris to see.

Chris leaned away from the injured man's bloody wound and cringed. "I don't know, but it doesn't look like the alcohol helped at all."

The engines growled as the plane sped down the runway for take-off.

"Maybe you should use something for a tourniquet," Chris suggested, still distancing himself from the festering arm. "I think it's spreading."

Seth's eyes widened and his jaw dropped. He turned his arm and watched as the skin split. With his uninjured hand, he yanked his backpack from underneath the seat and unclasped the top. His hand disappeared inside and rooted around the contents. When he pulled it out, his fingers were wrapped around a pair of panty-hose.

"Interesting choice, but that should work," Chris said. He took them and wound one of the legs just below Seth's elbow.

"These things aren't mine," Seth said. "They're from a stewardess on the last flight."

Chris raised an eyebrow and tied a knot in the stretchy fabric. "There," he said. "That should help."

The dripping lessened as the seatbelt light darkened. Seth released his seatbelt and strode toward the front of the plane. Chris unbuckled and situated the earbuds from his MP3 player. Making an attempt for a more comfortable seat, he pressed the recline button. Nothing happened. Straining his neck, he found the seat back pressed against the back wall of the cabin. "So much for comfort," he mumbled.

Pressing his pillow onto the window, he leaned against it and closed his eyes. He let his music block the screaming children, chattering passengers, and engine drone.

Seth dropped back into his seat, then poked Chris in the arm. "Hey. You awake?" he asked.

Chris yawned and lifted his head from the pillow. He plucked an earbud and turned to stare at Seth.

"Look at this." Seth lifted his bandaged arm. "Tammy used half the first aid kit on me."

His arm was wrapped in what looked like several rolls of white gauze, which was turning pink from the blood still seeping from the wound. He pulled an orange prescription bottle from his bag and strained with the childproof cap. When he pried it open, some of the pills spilled onto the seat.

"She said she'd come back and help me out in a while." Seth sneered and wriggled his eyebrows before popping two pills into his mouth and swallowing them dry. He closed the lid and re-placed the tube in his bag. "Until then, these puppies should take the edge off."

Seth slipped off his boots and stretched his legs into the walk-way. As his breathing drifted into snores, Chris wrinkled his nose. A rotten odor wafted into his nostrils. He scanned the area for the source of the stench and saw Seth's lonesome shoes, then cringed.

Seth let out a snorting grunt when Chris jostled his arm in an attempt to wake him. Beads of sweat had bloomed on Seth's forehead, and a line of drool hung from the corner of his mouth. After the fifth arm punch, Chris gave up trying to rouse him. He pulled his t-shirt over his mouth and huddled by the window, resting his head on his pillow. Resuming his music, he drowned out the increasing volume of Seth's disgruntled sleep.

After several mid-80's pop songs, Chris felt a light tap on his arm, and turned to see Tammy leaning toward him. Her shirt was unbuttoned just enough to reveal the hint of a black lace bra. He pulled his shirt down from his nose, plucked an earbud from his ear, and looked her in the eye.

"Would you like a drink, sir?" she asked; her eye flicked sideways to glimpse Seth's reclining form.

"Just some ice water if you have any."

Tammy nodded and scooped some ice into a plastic cup. She twisted off the cap of a small plastic water bottle and poured. After passing the container over the twitching sleeper, she smiled and trundled the cart back up the aisle.

Chris sipped his drink and twisted his face when he caught a whiff of his seatmate's feet. They smelled more like decaying meat than sweaty socks. He'd heard that what a person ate determined how his feet smelled. From the rising stench, Chris figured Seth had eaten garbage and drank from the gutter.

At least he stopped snoring, Chris thought as he returned to his music. He sighed and watched the snowcapped mountains below him. When they gave way to the Midwestern plains, Seth punched him in the arm. When Chris turned, he found Seth thrashing in his seat.

"Hey, man, you're having a nightmare," Chris said and shook Seth's arm to wake him.

Seth's skin was cold and pasty. He opened his bloodshot eyes as Tammy strutted by to the back of the cabin. When the flight attendant neared, he stood up, grabbed her, and pushed her into the cramped bathroom stall.

Tammy giggled as the door closed behind them. Chris shook his head and turned again to stare out the window at the ground below.

"We should lock this." Tammy's voice filtered through the flimsy panel a moment before the slider moved to *Occupied*.

A dull thumping sounded against the partition, and a whispered *yes* slithered from the tiny compartment.

Then, Tammy screamed.

A tidal flow of turning heads spanned the length of the plane as Tammy's shrieks escalated in volume. The other flight attendant sprinted toward the closed door as the cries tapered to a gurgling whimper, then silence.

"Tammy?" The woman slapped her palm against the small door. "Tammy, what's going on in there?" Her question was met with muffled thumps and the sound of tearing fabric. She pressed her ear to the door to hear better.

Chris watched as she jerked her head back and stared at the closed door. Stepping back, she dropped into the vacant seat next to him.

"Is Tammy okay?" Chris asked.

The flight attendant spun to face him. Her nametag hung at an odd angle. He had to tilt his head sideways to read *Jillian*. Her eyes widened, and her mouth made suffocating fishlike movements.

"I...I...can't tell," she said. Lowering her head and flicking her gaze back to the closed door, she added, "I came back here because of the screams, but now it's quiet." Jillian stood and smoothed her skirt. She stepped forward and tapped on the door with a white tipped fingernail, then leaned her face to the sealed crack of the door. "Tammy," she said in a stage whisper. "I'm gonna open the door if you don't answer me by the time I count to five."

Several peering heads dropped out of sight as passengers returned to their own business.

"One….two…"

A few parents pulled their children into forward-facing seated positions.

"You don't want me to get your mother from First Class, do you?" one man said before the child beside him disappeared.

"Three…four…"

Chris eyed the door warily as something dragged down the inside wall of the lavatory.

"Five." Jillian took a deep breath. "Okay, Tammy. I'm coming in."

She flipped up the small lavatory sign. She glanced to the plane full of people before sliding the knob into the *Vacant* position. Gripping the handle, she opened the door and stared in horror. One of her hands flew to cover the gasp that escaped from her mouth as the other shot forward in a desperate attempt to close the door.

Seth tumbled through the opening. Blood covered the front of his body. A chunk of flesh hung from his mouth. The pin from Tammy's nametag poked through his cheek. He grunted once and threw himself at Jillian, who still attempted to block his exit.

Chris jumped to his feet, knocking his head against the luggage bin and dropping back into his seat before regaining his footing. He leaned around the struggling flight attendant and threw a quick punch at the flailing maniac. Unphased by the jab to his jaw, Seth continued to grapple and snap his teeth at Jillian's arms.

Chris pushed the woman away from Seth's groping hands. Jillian shrieked and grabbed her forearm as she fell. Chris lifted his boot and kicked Seth in the chest, who toppled backwards into the small lavatory and slipped in the wetness on the floor. Reaching for the door to slam it shut, Chris stopped when he saw the state of the tiny room. Crimson streaks ran from the ceiling to the floor. Maroon puddles covered the floor and sink. Once blond hair, now stringy pink, hung in patches across a gaping bite mark in Tammy's face. Her remaining eye stared at the pink-hued light filtering through the gore-covered fixture. A lump of intestines trailed into the toilet bowl from her torn stomach.

Seth struggled to rise, and Chris closed and locked the lavatory door, using the hidden mechanism under the sign. Just before he closed it, he thought he saw Tammy's limp hand clench into a fist.

Jillian was sitting in the aisle with her hand wrapped around her wrist. Blood seeped from beneath her palm. Tears streamed down her cheeks, her bottom lip quivering. An old woman sitting across the aisle patted the flight attendant's shoulder with a liver-spotted hand. Long strands of yellow yarn trailed to the floor from a mound of string in her lap.

"Jillian, are you okay?" Chris asked, feeling stupid for saying it as soon as the words left his lips.

"Does she look okay?" the older woman asked in a shrill whisper. "She's bleeding all over herself. She needs a doctor."

"Do you see a doctor anywhere?" Chris glanced around the immediate area. Most of the other passengers either stared directly at them, or out the windows to avoid direct contact with the drama unfolding next to their seats. No one wanted to get involved and Chris didn't blame them.

"Is there a doctor on the plane?" the old woman shouted.

A few heads turned to look before shaking their heads and returning to their own endeavors.

"No," Jillian said. The word emerged through a short sob. "There aren't any doctors or nurses on the flight."

"That's all right, dear," the old woman said. "I was a nurse along time ago." Grabbing the seat in front of her, the old woman pulled herself into a stooped slouch. "I'll take care of you. Just show me to the first aid kit."

"Let's get you on your feet," Chris said to Jillian.

He placed a hand under her elbow and helped her stand. Still clutching her arm, Jillian wiped her dripping nose on her sleeve. She teetered on sensible heels before stabilizing.

"Don't you worry, Nurse Tobin is here." The old woman wrapped a bony arm around Jillian's waist. "We'll get you fixed right up."

The two hobbled toward the front of the plane.

"Don't worry about me," Chris muttered. "I'll keep the situation contained."

He glanced at the closed lavatory door. The door shuddered. He scanned the area and reached under Mrs. Tobin's seat. A hand-carved eagle topped the slender wooden shaft of her cane.

Fumbling through the tangle of yarn, he unwound a set of metal knitting needles. He idly wondered how the old woman had managed to get the knitting needles onto the plane, and figured she had played the weak old lady and had fooled airport security when being searched for contraband.

A thump sounded when he returned to the lavatory. The red *Occupied* flag showed through the slot. A miniscule amount of green for *Vacant* peeked at the edge.

Chris lifted the flap and pressed the lever back into the locked position. He dropped onto the hard seat cushion and held the cane ready to jab anything that might escape.

Two distinct voices moaned and growled from inside the lavatory. In Chris' mind, there had been no chance that the flight attendant could have survived her injuries. Parts of her insides had been scattered in the corners of the tiny stall. The thin door panel shuddered as four fists pounded on the surface. The red sign shifted.

"Who's in there?" a man asked as he stepped up to the door. Lifting his fist, he knocked. "Finish up. Other people are waiting."

More of the red slid to green.

"That's not a good idea," Chris said.

The man turned and stared, open-mouthed, at Chris.

"I've been waiting for twenty minutes. I can't wait any longer for these two no-class losers to join some club." He kicked the door with a tasseled loafer. "Let me in!"

Chris could hear fingernails scrabbling at the edge of the door as the slide exposed more of the green *Vacant*. Then the door popped open and blood encrusted arms shot through the gap.

Twisted, bloody fingers clutched the disgruntled man's shirt as he shrieked and tried to escape.

Using the cane, Chris beat back the grasping hands. The man tumbled to the floor and scrambled up the aisle, mumbling incoherent sounds of terror.

Chris gripped the handle on the door and tried to close it, but too many body parts blocked him. The door opened wider and Tammy's torso flopped into the aisle. She snarled up at Chris as Seth reached toward him.

Chris kicked the hissing dead woman in the face as he ducked out of Seth's grasp. He pressed the cane into the man's chest and shoved him back into the doorway.

The opening wasn't wide enough to accommodate Seth's awkward stance. Chris felt fingers wrap around his ankle. Reaching into his back pocket, he grabbed a knitting needle and thrust it into Tammy's remaining eye.

The orb exploded in a pinkish ooze as the needle slid through the eye socket and into her brain. Her body slumped into a limp pool of flesh.

The seats ahead of the struggling figures emptied as passengers scurried to distance themselves from the melee, all screaming in fear and terror. Chris continued to stab the walking stick into Seth's solar plexus.

"This is your captain speaking," a voice mumbled through the overhead speakers. "Please return to your seats. Due to unforeseen circumstances, we're required to make an unscheduled landing in Chicago."

Seth's body shifted and the door opened wider. The tall man fell into the lavatory. The top of his head smashed into the metal toilet bowl, his neck snapping to hang at an odd angle. His body lay still in the congealing puddles of Tammy's guts.

Chris tapped the dead man with the tip of the cane. Other than jostling him, the body remained motionless.

Dragging the back of his wrist across his forehead, Chris sighed heavily.

"Are they dead?" a woman's voice asked from behind him. It was high-pitched and filled with panic.

"I think so," Chris said as he continued to stare at the bodies.

"What was wrong with them?" a man asked. "Are they terrorists?"

Chris shrugged and curled back into his window seat. The orderly grid of landing strips loomed beneath the plane as it banked to land. "No, it's not that."

"This is your captain speaking," the voice crackled once more in the speakers. "Please place your trays in their upright positions and fasten your seatbelts."

The old woman who had helped Jillian shuffled back to her seat as the other passengers scurried to strap themselves in for landing, all talking animatedly amongst themselves.

A smattering of clicks sounded as the aircraft bounced down the runway a few minutes later.

As the plane taxied toward the terminal, Chris peered through a crack in the lavatory door. Seth hadn't moved. The splashes of blood glinted in the fluorescent glow.

Jillian trundled down the aisle and slumped into Seth's abandoned seat. Her forehead glistened with droplets of perspiration. A pink splotch had soaked through the gauze covering the wound on her arm.

"Are you all right?" he asked.

"I'll be fine," Jillian said, leaning back on the headrest and closing her eyes. "I'm just really tired. Once this is over, I'm gonna sleep like the dead." She coughed and closed her eyes.

Chris smelled road kill each time the flight attendant exhaled. Her arm twitched, and her breath rattled in her chest. He rolled his eyes and reached into the pocket on the seat in front of him.

Sliding the remaining slender knitting needle out from his back pocket, he hid it between the pages of a SkyMall magazine, then gripped it to his chest.

Pressing his back against the window, he waited for Jillian's breathing to stop.

ABOUT THE WRITERS

Dana Bell is a Colorado writer who is well traveled and often incorporates regional settings into her stories. Her first novel "Winter Awakening" from WolfSinger Publications is available on Amazon. She has stories in several anthologies, listed on her fanfiction profile page, and poems in magazines. She lives with her husband David Luperti who is a nature photographer and three cats Sammy, Maximillian and Adara. Building and decorating doll houses is her main hobby along with writing fanficiton under the name Dragonlots.

See more of her work at www.fanfiction.net/~dragonlots.

Alyn Day is a member of the New England Horror Writers and an avid horror enthusiast with an inclination towards zombies. She enjoys sushi, gaming, and participating in various zombie walks around the Boston Area. Follow her exploits and adventures on twitter: http://twitter.com/#!/Z0mbiegrl

Gretchen Elhassani is torn in many different directions. She has two jobs, two children, a house, a husband, and is sporadically taking classes towards a Bachelor's Degree. She has one novel published, THE LINCOLN LETTER, and is working with Rainstorm Press on a second novel, THE SILVER CONSPIRACY.

Jennifer Goraczkowski is an aspiring Fantasy writer who completed her first novel in 2010. Though it has not been published, she is actively submitting her manuscript. She's lived in Colorado Springs for most of her life and enjoys spending time with family and friends. She's been a member of the Colorado Springs Fiction Writers group for just over a year and has learned a great deal from its members. Jennifer is an avid reader of fantasy and enjoys writing it as well.

Chauma Smith Guss, the only actual true believer in the family, can be found late at night reading post-apocalyptic fiction of all sorts with the covers pulled over her head and the machete within reach.

Jennifer Koehler lives and works in Ohio. Her short story "The Lonely Vampire" was published in Post Mortem Press' "Mon Coeur Mort." She looks forward to publishing more short stories in the future.

J.L. Petty is an award winning fiction writer. Most of her short stories range in contemporary horror, suspense, science fiction, and fantasy fiction. Her most recent short stories are included in *Death and the Journalist, Tales of the Dead: A Zombie Anthology,* and *Daily Flash 2012: 366 Days of Flash Fiction.*

Suzanne Robb's debut novel "Z-Boat" will be released by Twisted Library Press under their Library of the Living Dead Imprint. Her stories are in current and upcoming anthologies with various publishers such as Coscom Entertainment, Twisted Library Press, Post Mortem Press, Pill Hill Press, Wicked East Press, Rymfire eBooks, Norgus Press, May December Publications, Living Dead Press, and Hidden Thoughts Press. In her free time she reads, watches movies, plays with her dog, and enjoys chocolate and Legos. http://suzannerobb.blogspot.com/

Katie Simmons is a fiction writer residing outside of Pittsburgh, Pennsylvania. Her true passion is writing western novels, but recently she switched to writing short stories and has a few published in various genres.

Marilyn Simpson writes dark, surreal and horror fiction. She lives in England with her cat and imaginary friends. She dreams a lot and turns her dreams into enchanting tales. She's currently working on her first novel, A Dark Romance.

Julianne Snow: It was while watching Romero's *Night of the Living Dead* at age six that she solidified her respect of the undead. Since that day, she's been preparing herself for the (inevitable) Zombpocalypse. While classically trained in all of the ways to defend herself, she took up writing in order to process the desire she now covets; to bestow a second and final death upon the undead. Her first book "Days with the Undead: Book One" was released in early 2012 and while based on her web serial of the same name, it's inherently creepier and vividly poignant.

Rebecca Snow lives in Virginia with a well-traveled husband and a group of flightless cats. Her short fiction has been published in a number of small press anthologies. She can be found online at cemeteryflower.blog.com and on Twitter@cemeteryflower.

Candis Vargo was born in Lufkin, Texas but raised in Rome, Pennsylvania where she resides with her husband and children. After she married her high-school-sweetheart and realized she was living a Romance Novel of her own, she decided to create more stories to share with others. Her love for the undead formed when her friend Stephanie, cast her into a world of endless book exchanges, watching vampires and killing zombies, and for that she grateful.

You can learn more about her at www.candisvargo.com

NEW HORROR FICTION FROM OPEN CASKET PRESS!

HEADSHOTS ONLY: A ZOMBIE ANTHOLOGY

Edited by Anthony Giangregorio

The walking dead cannot be stopped!

They never tire, never give up, and will come for you again and again!

Only one thing can put them down for good!

Grab your gun, take aim, and make sure it's a head shot!

One to the brain pan is the only way to save yourself from certain death!

So keep your weapon loaded, stay sharp, and remember…*Headshots Only!*

HOLLOW POINT: A ZOMBIE NOVEL

By Mark Christopher

Something horrible is happening in the small, bayou town of Cypress Pass. The dead are walking.

Caught in the middle of the undead uprising is Sheriff John Boudreaux; a retired Army Ranger, who still struggles daily with the emotional and physical pain of his time in the Iraq war.

Now he finds himself fighting an enemy that cannot be stopped, an enemy that shows no fear and wants nothing more than to eat his flesh. He's tasked with a mission that will define his life. He must save his friends and fight off the living dead that are overrunning his town. But how do you kill what is already dead?

CREATURE FEATURE: A MONSTER ANTHOLOGY

Edited by Anthony Giangregorio

Giant squirrels, massive zombies, killer trees and marauding severed heads are just a few of the twisted tales of creatures you will find inside this anthology.

So let your imagination free and embrace what isn't real.

For perhaps monsters are real, and it is you that does not truly exist.

HORROR CARNIVAL

Edited by Anthony Giangregorio

Step right up, folks, the Horror Carnival is about to begin!

We have a great show in store for you this evening.

Ghouls, monsters, zombies, vampires and serial killers, all rolled up into one massive show. Tales that will leave you wanting more yet leave you oh so fulfilled.

The rides are cheap, the stories tall, so grab some cotton candy and popcorn and enjoy yourself. Tickets are five for a dollar!

But please read all disclaimers before entering the fairgrounds.

Horror Carnival is not responsible for any dismemberment or loss of organs during your visit, nor are we liable if any family member is slain while participating in one of the attractions. So come on in…if you dare!

ZOMBIE BUFFET: AN UNDEAD ANTHOLOGY

Edited by Anthony Giangregorio

If you're hungry for zombie stories, look no further than this anthology.

There's enough rotting meat to satisfy even the most discerning connoisseur, and our all-you-can-eat buffet is sure to please.

Rotting intestines, severed heads and exploding spleens are just some of the courses waiting for you within this book of undead mastication.

So grab a knife and fork, slap on a napkin, 'cause you're gonna get dirty, and prepare yourself for the Zombie Buffet.

A zombie feast of epic proportions.

DEAD CHRISTMAS: A ZOMBIE ANTHOLOGY

Edited by Anthony Giangregorio

Share the most special time of the year with someone you love, or better yet, with an animated corpse!

The living dead love Christmas. Whether they're hanging their entrails like garland, using severed heads like stockings, or hanging body parts like ornaments, even zombies enjoy the most wonderful time of the year.

Santa Claus isn't immune to the walking dead, either.

Zombie elves, killer reindeer and undead hordes, all seek to share in the joy of the holiday . . . and tear Santa apart and feed on his flesh.

So when you grab last year's fruitcake to re-gift to Aunt Martha, just make sure to bring a shotgun, too. Because for all you know, your aunt has turned into an undead flesh-eater, and if the shotgun won't kill her, the fruitcake most assuredly will.

RATS

By Anthony Giangregorio

Killer black rats the size of dogs are roaming the streets and no one is aware of their existence.

Wild dogs, the authorities warn. Stay indoors and all will be fine.

Domenic Salvatore soon finds himself in the middle of a cover-up of epic proportions; where no one will believe the truth.

And why would they? After all, he's just a kid.

What no one knows is that the rats have taken on a taste for human meat, a particular kind of meat actually…young flesh…the flesh of children.

As the kids are hunted one by one, killed and dragged off into the night to be devoured, Domenic realizes that it's only a matter of time before he's next.

Something evil stalks the town of Wakefield, Mass…and it's hungry.

BIGFOOT TALES

Edited by Mark Christopher

The elusive Bigfoot has been a mystery for years.

Truth or hoax? No one knows for sure and perhaps never will.

So does this creature of the forest truly exist? Is there really a missing link that ties together man with his ape ancestors?

Or is it all simply a figment of the imagination.

ZOMBIES, MONSTERS, CREATURES OF THE NIGHT

OPEN CASKET PRESS

OPEN CASKET PRESS.COM

THE NEW NAME IN HORROR

UNDEAD PRESS

UNDEADPRESS.COM

THE PLACE TO GO FOR ZOMBIE AND APOCALYPTIC FICTION

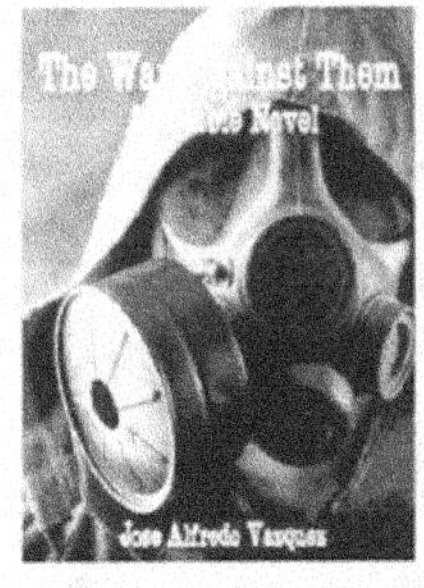

LIVING DEAD PRESS

WHERE THE DEAD WALK
www.livingdeadpress.com

CLAN OF THE BIGFOOT

ANTHONY GIANGREGORIO

www.ingramcontent.com/pod-product-compliance
Lightning Source LLC
Chambersburg PA
CBHW070500120726

47910CB00003B/1078